Arranged Lives

[Edited]

A Novel by Lee Zappulla

PRELUDE

Eleven-year-old Nina's three years away from her family made her forget their unusual way of life. Her family sought to take advantage of the multiple trauma's impact on her memory. Nina's stolen diary jeopardized the careers of two medical doctors connected with her family. Her entire family faced disgrace and shame for the year they abandoned her after her accident, and to be used as a guinea pig for new and untested medical treatments. The family isolated her for two years after parents reclaimed her for outpatient continued care. The families took advantage of the Catholic church's generosity and charity in paying for Nina's medical care, for her hospital, surgical, and out-patient care.

Nina was twenty-five years old when her divorced father, Michael, broke The Family Code of Silence to help her remember life before the accident. He told her he felt the motivation behind her hospitalized accident was for her to die. He told her about the family's jealousy towards other family. Several members of Nina's family helped her to overcome her disbelief regarding what her father said, and none of them addressed her father's encouragement for Nina to write a book about her life.

From that point forward, Nina was bombarded by confusion, frustration, harassment, and trouble of all kinds. One therapist confessed that he was part of her family's activities. Some of what he told matched what her father said two decades earlier. The therapist advised her to sever ties with her dysfunctional family. But Nina needed more proof about her life and the family she grew up with. She consulted with priests unconnected to her family, to avoid the relatives who had joined the priesthood.

The first priest said, "Such lifetime activities don't happen even in Italy unless there's sickness." Nina needed to figure out the family's sickness and if more than one sickness.

A missionary said, "I've never heard of any family situation as complicated as yours. Knowing where, how, and with whom to begin help is a challenge." Now, Nina needed to also figure out how to explain her complicated family life.

A semi-retired priest said, "I've known only one family like yours. Their activities didn't end until the last of them died." Nina knew she needed to maintain limited contact with her estranged family in order to know when all of them died, leaving her as the sole living member.

The last priest Nina consulted with said he understood families like hers but wanted to know how they accomplished their goals. Although Nina did not visit this priest again, his words made her remember that her father said one goal of the family was to win use of the person's free will. He added that the power of suggestion and brainwashing accomplished the same result. He said tricks with free will left a person with only self to blame for what life held. The end goal was for the person to accept that they were to blame for what happened in their life.

Meet the People

In their Italian country parts, Donald and his family enjoyed the honor, prestige and advantages of their family name that was the name of a city and on maps of Italy. Bachelor Donald's drinking and gambling habits created debts that his family paid to not disgrace their family name. Shortly after Donald and Patricia married each other, she was pregnant. Donald's family practiced the rule to *take care of their own.* They now worried about onward life after Patricia gave birth and likelihood that their marriage would produce more children. Donald's sisters Phyllis and Susan believed that gossip about his behavior troubled their ability to find suitable husbands. Families of Donald and Patricia held a meeting in which they decided to send this married couple out of Italy to America. Donald's sisters Phyllis and Susan would travel with them. Doctor Andrew would also travel with them to be on hand when his sister Patricia delivers her first child.

Donald, Patricia and their separate families were from the northern Sicily, but their family names were carried to other parts of Sicily and into America. Family of Donald and Patricia did not pursue people with their family name who settled in America to be sponsors. Donald and siblings wanted to hold on to the honor, prestige and advantages with their family name and didn't want to accidentally be associated with who disgraced their family name in America. They planned to keep maps of Italy with their family name on it to show people they met in America.

The first child of Donald and Patricia was a girl born on ocean waters near to America. She was named Jean and considered to be an American citizen. Donald and Patricia produced four more children. He was employed in a barber shop. His continued gambling and drinking always hurt his ability to provide for his family, He continued to rely on the past practices of his family who practiced that *families take care of their own.* For the sake of his continued and/or new employment as well as keeping a clean family name, Donald's sisters [Phyllis and Susan] with the help of Doctor Andrew paid his gambling and drinking debts

 Doctor Andrew's work as a medical doctor continued successfully in America. He cared for Patricia's additional four child births and her miscarriage without a fee. And provided family of Donald and Patricia with ongoing medical care without fees.

Susan was a seamstress in a factory. She married an Italian co-worker who settled in America years earlier. After hours in wage paying work, duties as housekeeper and homemaker, she made clothes for the children of Donald and Patricia with size changes as the children grew.

Phyllis married Donald's coworker, an Italian man who settled in America years earlier. Phyllis and husband homesteaded land they made into farmlands from which Phyllis contributed poultry, cow's milk, fruits and vegetables to Donald's family.

Phyllis, Susan and Doctor Andrew shared the costs of footwear and school supplies for the growing children of Donald and Patricia.

Nothing said and done made Donald a responsible provider for his family. Their families would not send them with their children back to Italy. If done, the shame and losing face reactions for Phyllis, Susan and Doctor Andrew would prevent them from trips to Italy to visit family there. Phyllis, Susan and Doctor Andrew felt that Donald took advantage of and abused their family practice to *take care of their own*, but did not know how to change the situation.

* * * * * * * * * * * * *

Widowed Emily's family consisted of twenty-year-old daughter Laura, eighteen-year-old son Wayne, fourteen-year-old son Michael, and twelve-year-old son Lance. Their family included unofficially adopted fourteen-year-old Linda, an only child for owners of the nearby farmland. Linda's parents allowed her to spend every day with Emily's family so she could be with other children. Emily treated Linda as if one of her children and gave her farmland duties as given to the others. At the end of a day's work, Linda introduced games that challenged them all in some way. They were games Linda never played before but won all games with a big smile and look that silently said she could win and outwit them all at any time in life. She had no musical talents but sat quietly with Emily's family when Michael entertained them with his violin and his accordion.

Linda joined Emily and her four children to the town center to sell farm grown produce and shop for what they needed at home. It was a time of day when all other children were in school. Linda, Michael and Lance ran about in ways that disturbed many of the townspeople who went to the town mayor's office with complaints about these three children. The mayor asked his assistant to find and bring these children and their parents to him. Laura told the mayor that her mother had a very sore throat and would speak on her behalf. Laura answered the mayor's questions and informed him they had no telephone. She was given a pencil and blank sheet of paper to write their home address.

In less than a week, representatives of the school system visited Emily's home. They learned that Emily's family and Linda lived in an isolated part of the city that wasn't searched for school aged children. The mayor and close school officials worried about affects if the situation became gossip that travelled to other townspeople and to upper school officials who might charge them with negligence of duty and terminate their employment. They decided to send Emily and her family to America after Wayne and Michael were prepared for employment there. The mayor and school officials viewed Emily and children as a tight knit family, with Linda an unofficial part of it. It was learned that Laura had some years of formal schooling before the family moved to the isolated country part. Also, that Laura used the Bible to help younger siblings and Linda learn how to read, write and about the world.

The mayor and school officials concluded that Emily's family unit would continue to take care of each other wherever situated. With the knowledge that America constantly constructed new buildings, they felt it right to teach Wayne and Michael mason skills. The financial budgets of the mayor's office and school system would pay costs of reservations on the boat to America for Emily and her four biological children. Some cash would be given to tide them until they found a place to live and employment. Linda could not be part of these expenses.

Linda's mother had a sister in America whose marriage produced only one child: Bertha. Linda's parents paid her costs to travel with Emily's family to America where Linda would become part of her aunt's family. Linda and Bertha were born a few days apart in the same month of the same year. Bertha allowed Linda to take a *big sister* role that Linda wanted.

In America, Laura was employed in a sewing factory; she married an Italian co-worker who settled in America two years earlier. They became homesteaders who kept chicken, cows for milk, and grew a variety of fruits and vegetables. They became neighbors of Donald's sister Phyllis and husband who settled as homesteaders two years earlier. Laura and Phyllis became friends who told each other about their lives before and since they made America home. Laura's talk about her family included unofficially adopted Linda and Linda's cousin Bertha.

When Bertha reached marriage age, she and Wayne married each other. Linda wanted to be a real part of the family she grew with and whom Bertha married into but Michael refused to have Linda as his bride. Linda told Michael he would someday regret having rejected her, no matter how long it took. She married Michael's coworker in mason work: Paul, an Italian man who settled in America years earlier.

Wayne and Bertha used her wedding dowry for a business that employed his brothers Michael and Lance. Savings from wages would allow Michael and Lance to buy partnership shares of this business that made men's hats they sold in their own retail shop and produced for other retailers of men's hats. As profits and the number of customers grew, their business added pickup and delivery services for clients, followed with cleaning and repair of men's hats. With continued business growth, they added men's accessories: ties, tie pins, neck scarves, earmuffs, gloves, socks, wallets, and cuff links.

Lance made trips to and from the nearby big city for wholesale prices of all things needed for their business operations. Wayne cut fabric for the hats. Michael shaped the hats on a mold. Bertha hand-stitched each hat with an inner lining, a brim trim, and a headband into which she tucked a small feather. The four of them quickly became very wealthy people with no time to own property and the work with it. Long hours with the business didn't allow Michael and Lance time needed to search for brides. They continued to live with their widowed mother near to where Wayne and Bertha lived.

Linda Used Victor's Free Will

Linda's wages as a factory seamstress and Paul's wages as a luncheonette cook

covered everyday living costs with very little savings for the unexpected. Shelly and

Linda were co-workers who became friends. Linda's talks about owning a business

brought Shelly's talk about Victor, a benefactor for who needed help to start a business.

Linda asked for, and Shelly told her how to contact Victor for help to start a business. At

the end of the workday, Linda telephoned Victor. She informed him that she was a co-

worker and friend of Shelly who recommended him for help to start a business. Linda and

Paul kept the appointment Victor scheduled. Victor was a tall, large boned, overweight

man with a strong but kind voice and strong handshake. All were comfortably seated in

his spacious home office when Victor explained the many books on a table in a corner: "I

keep records of who I helped to start a business. It includes the dates I checked their

business progress, the agreed upon repayment schedules, and payments made. When both

of you and I agree to connect with each other, your names would be part of these

books."

Linda told Victor, "Shelly believed you could help my husband and me to start a

food serving business. Paul's employment as a cook in a local eatery made him aware of

food serving business operations. Marriage helped me to cook a variety of meals that differ from what Paul does as a paid cook. I was an only child but since very young I was part of a large family in which Laura was like a big sister for me while the older sister of three younger brothers. She taught the four of us to read, write, arithmetic and about the world. Years with that family taught me how to relate to people, and this makes it easy for me to connect with people as a business owner, as a waitress and as a cashier. I believe Paul and I have all the qualifications needed to make a success in a food serving business."

Victor said, "Shelly told me to expect a call from you. I trust Shelly's judgement and referrals. She and I know each other for many years. She made clothes for my mother until her death last year. I helped Shelly to open her own sewing factory in which she always worked as if an employee. But now, let's get to how I might help you start a business."

Paul confirmed and added to what Linda told Victor: "We'd like a food serving business. Linda and I would devote full time to it when opened to the public. Linda would be waitress and cashier while I work in the kitchen. Our current meager savings may be enough for only a minor unexpected health issue. Savings are not enough for us to quit employment to devote full time to the business before it succeeds. Your help would be needed in every way."

"The two of you have what's needed for a food serving business. I need details about the size and type of store you want, where and how the customer and kitchen areas are to be set up, what equipment and furniture is wanted, and all else to make it your business."

"My wife is the talker. The nod of my head would confirm her details."

Victor continued. "Shelly said Linda is an employee who earned more than one bonus as the most productive worker. Good referrals allow me to trust who I help."

Linda needed no time to think about details. "We need you to find a ground level store with off-street, wide double door entrance. We want big glass windows at both sides of glass filled entrance doors. There must be windows in the kitchen, overhead lighting throughout the place, plus lighting outside the front and back doors. The restaurant name would be *Paul and Linda's Home Cooking* painted in big black letters on a front window. The customer area would be in the store front, and big enough for six tables that each seat four people with space for me to get to and around customers. We want a counter with stools to face the wall and seat six people. The counter should have room for a cash register near to the front doors. We want a coin operated public telephone in the customer area for their convenience and incoming calls to us.

"We believe our business would grow with a need to hire people. This means the kitchen must have space for more than two people to move about freely in it. The kitchen needs a variety of appliances and other things: two large refrigerators with freezers, a large cooking range with an oven, a large separate oven, sinks in which to wash produce and another for handwashing between handling of different foodstuff. Also needed are food preparation and food serving tools. The kitchen windows must be at normal levels for incoming light and at high level to let out heat and smoke. We need cabinets with drawers and shelves for dinnerware, eating and cooking utensils, tablecloths, napkins, eating and cooking utensils. More than one big pantry would be needed to store foodstuff plus a closet for cleaning items. We would need all things ready to open our business to the public before we quit wage paying work."

Victor looked to Paul. "I've seen your nods of agreement, but I want your spoken words for all your wife has said."

Paul responded, "Yes. I agree with all my wife said to you. She always planned our lives and our marriage has always worked well this way."

Victor said, "As Linda spoke, I drew a big picture of a store that is now vacant. I want both of you to mark where my team of workers should install the appliances, cabinets, storage closets and other things. When done, I want you both to individually sign this paper."

Linda marked the diagram of an empty store with where she wanted things placed. She and Paul then signed this.

After Victor studied the marked picture, he said, "Let us make sure that the three of us understand all involved: I am to find an empty store for your business, pay advance rental and deposit, arrange for and pay deposits and charges for utilities, arrange for installation of a coin operated telephone. I'm to advance funds for your choice of paint that my workers would put on the walls, ceilings, and store front window. I am to advance costs of floor covering, furniture, appliances, cabinets and equipment of your choice that workers would install. Also, to advance costs for your choice of dinnerware, cookware, utensils to prepare and serve food, tables, chairs, a customer counter, counter stools, tablecloths, napkins, cleaning items, and a cash register. My workers would also paint the restaurant name on a business front window with black paint.

"I would be on hand for deliveries to your business store while you both are at wage paid employment. At the end of your workday, one of you must check the list of delivered items and, sign the receipts for all purchased. One of you must check a list of work that my employees did, their time at the listed hourly pay, plus my time and services on your behalf---then sign it as another part of my records. All records should show the dollar amount due me. I would open a repayment schedule when your business shows steady net profits that are sufficient for continued business operations."

Linda and Paul simultaneously said, "It sounds complete. When and how would we know when to quit employment to start as business owners with doors opened for customers?"

"At scheduled times, the three of us would meet at the business site to check that progress is to your satisfaction. You give employers notice that you quit when all is done to open your business doors to the public. Have I covered everything?"

Paul said, "If this happens, if all is possible our business start couldn't be easier."

"Yes, all is possible. With both of you working full time at this business, I believe it would prove profitable in three months after opened for the public. For a minimum of three months, I would advance repayable funds to cover business expenses. From now to then, it's your duty to save from continued wages for personal living costs. After your business is opened to the public, I'd make monthly reviews of your financial activity records with a copy of it for my records signed by both of you. Again, is all clear to and understood by both of you?"

Paul and Linda separately responded with the same words: "I understand all said and planned between us."

Victor added, "Keep in mind that you must keep records of business financial activities for yearly federal and state tax returns as well as for my records."

One month after the business opened to the public, Linda told Victor, "We can't succeed in this location where there's minimal traffic of people and no public transportation. On my trips to the farmlands I saw a vacant store with a telephone number for information on its big front window. I wrote that telephone number on this piece of paper. The store is ground level of an apartment building; to its right and left are big tenement buildings. It's across the street from the start and end of bus and trolley car public transportation. That depot is walking distance to and from farmlands where people shop. Customers and business profits would be quick and steady for us in that location."

Victor said, "It sounds ideal for your business, but . . .."

Linda interrupted. "My cousin Bertha and husband Wayne used her wedding dowry for a business with his two brothers. Their business was a quick success and made the four of them very wealthy people. The family Bertha married into and I grew up together in Italy. I don't like being the only poor one among them. I confessed being jealous of them. I told them Paul and I would also become wealthy and maybe wealthier than they are. Jealousy is my driving force!"

Victor responded, "The Bible does say no one could stand before jealousy. I need

your husband's confirmation that he agrees with the new business location. Also, that you

both understand that relocating your business would increase your debt to me?"

Paul and Linda individually said the same thing: "We want the new business

location and understand it would increase your costs to help us."

With a moving truck, Victor and his workers moved things out of the first store

and into the truck. Before leaving the site, Victor's workers repaired holes in the walls

and ceilings after removal of various items. If floor covering was removed, it would leave

a bare wood floor; thus, none was removed. When at the new location, all things were

removed from the truck and the men repeated all done in and at the first location.

This business location quickly made Linda and Paul wealthy business owners.

Victor was in this eatery with a repayment schedule for them. Paul was silent while Linda ———

refused to sign it. "We owe nothing for your help to start this business. Its success has

been our hard work and long hours. You helped your countrymen, and nothing is owed

for doing what the Bible instructs."

Victor was on a counter stool facing Linda and Paul as he told them, "The Bible

also says an *eye for eye* and *do unto others as you'd have them do unto you*. How would

you feel if you were unpaid benefactors?" Victor used these words from the Bible

without premeditated plans. He calmly said *goodbye* as he walked out the business front

doors.

Linda proudly an unashamedly told the people she called family how she and Paul

became wealthy business owners. All family expressed great concern about punishment for refusal to repay Victor in any way.

Linda responded, "Nothing proved that Victor believed in any form of violence. If he uses the Bible's words about *free will*, we understand *free will* and are careful in all matters."

Kangaroo Court Help

Victor and Shelly became friends while she added to the wardrobe of his mother whose passing is now more than a year ago. Victor and Shelly continued to meet with each other on Saturdays at three in the afternoon in a diner where they had coffee and pie as they chatted. They were seated at a table when Shelly asked Victor, "How are Linda and Paul doing with the business you helped them start? Are they now on the books for repayment to you?"

Shelly didn't interrupt Victor as he uncomfortably told her about his help for Linda and Paul that ended with, "They were my first experience with people who seemed to be trustworthy and honorable but turned out to be the opposite. Linda used the Bible's words about help to countrymen and insisted it meant no repayment was due. She pointed out that no force was used for my help, and they signed nothing that made them responsible to repay me in any way. She again used the Bible to say I had the *free will* choice to do or not do what was done for them."

With a look of complete surprise, Shelly said, "You gave and did a lot more than what's normal. Linda made a fool of you! Refusal to repay any debt is a disgrace among their people and everyone else. Linda should not have used the Bible's words about *help thy countrymen* nor its words about *free will*. Linda must suffer what she made you suffer; it's a non-violent action called *eat your words and ways*. Work for this could use some of what Linda spoke about to me as we worked together in my sewing factory.

"Linda spoke about the family she was part of in Italy in growing years and traveled with them to restart life America. She continued life in America with her mother's sister and this aunt's only daughter Bertha. Wayne was the oldest man in family Linda grew up with in Italy and whom she has referred to as her family. When Bertha and Wayne married each other, they were given a big dowry that was used to start a men's hat business with his two brothers. That business made the four of them wealthy people and Linda didn't want to be the only poor one among them. With her confessed jealousy to them, she vowed that she and Paul would become wealthier than they were. All of this tells us that she doesn't want to be jealous of anyone and wants people jealous of her, and that she values money. Her use of me to connect with you indicates that she uses people. Her refusal to repay a debt let us know she plays with *free will*."

Victor interrupted, "How does all this make Linda *eat words and ways*, as you put it?"

"Please hear me out. I'm putting pieces of her life and ways together as done with jig saw puzzles. Wayne's only sister Laura was like a big sister for Linda in Italy. Laura and husband homesteaded land they made into a farming business. Their farmland neighbors were Phyllis and husband who homesteaded the land two years before Laura and husband did. Phyllis and Laura became friends who told each other about their lives before and after they left Italy. Linda was part of meetings held by the people she called family. In a family meeting Laura told them all about the problems of her neighbor Phyllis and siblings with their brother Donald. His gambling and drinking habits kept him from responsibilities as a husband and father of his five growing children. Donald and his family bettered life in America with their family name on maps of Italy they showed people. His overuse of it helped him to build drinking and gambling debts. To not disgrace their family name here, his family paid those debts. They also provided for his family with clothing and footwear while his wife's doctor brother medically cared for them. Phyllis and her siblings don't know how to free themselves of duty to *take good care of their* own without making life more painful for his wife and growing children."

Victor interrupted: "Shelly, how do you know so much about all these people?"

"It's talks from Linda to me. You and I know that some people refer to this as gossip. Linda shops for produce and other food items at the farmlands in that area and became friends with Phyllis."

"Okay but I don't understand how this all fits with how things go forward."

"You would understand when I tell you about what's called a Kangaroo Court. It would be people you've helped and meet with you monthly to make their scheduled repayments. Some of them fully repaid you but continue to attend the monthly gatherings to visit the others with whom a friendship grew. In the upcoming meeting, you tell them what you told me; their facial reactions would undoubtedly be as it was for me: surprise. You ask for their opinion about how to deal with Linda and Paul, or if you should take it as a lesson to not let it happen again."

"I don't want to sound like a cry baby. I don't want to come across stupid for having let this happen. What could come from what you call a Kangaroo Court if I do what you advise?"

"You won't sound like a cry baby or stupid. To start, I would stand in front of all at the meeting. All there know I'm someone you have helped to start a business. I would explain that you helped Linda and Paul to start a business based on my recommendation about her as my employee then. I'd then ask them all to listen to your experiences with help for them to start a business. After you personally detail it, I again stand in front of all there and give my suggestion, my belief that Linda and Paul should be punished without physical violence and no destruction of property. I would say punishment should fit words from the Bible that Linda used with refusal to repay you. I tell all at the meeting about a family who needs what's called *clean hands* help to end their help for the family of a brother with drinking and gambling debt and five growing children from three to thirteen years of age. The irresponsible brother comes across as a user. The plan would be to connect Linda and Paul with him and his family unit. It would mix opposites of all ways and things that the growing children would refuse to accept when marriage ages. The result would be that Linda was a benefactor whose free will helped her countrymen as the Bible instructs and loser without returns. Life made her *eat words and ways*."

Victor again interrupted, "It sounds like this Donald might feel his family would take of his family no matter what his mistakes or wrongs."

"Yes. He apparently played with his birth family's custom to *take care of their own*. After I present things at the meeting, you again speak. You confirm that you want no physical violence and no destruction of property. Also, that you want to work with the Bible's words that Linda used. You will be surprised how many of them would say Linda made a fool of you and should suffer a like experience. In this meeting, it's important for the group to know that Linda told you jealousy was her driving force. Also, about her pride and big ego with business success that made her and Paul wealthier than who she called family. All things would help to direct the activities to go forward. All done by this

Kangaroo Court would let no fingers point to you or people who share in the work. You

continue a friendship with Linda and Paul as an occasional customer. This lets you know

how much of what's been arranged is working or has worked. You and others in the

activities would report to who is designated as the chief for further instructions that keep

things moving forward. The power of suggestion and brainwashing do the same work.

Your part of things would be to suggest that Linda appoint herself matriarch of the people

she calls family and answer her question about the duties in such a role. Other people in

our activities would buy foodstuff from the farmlands owned by Laura and Paul and

Phyllis and husband. People from our group would develop a friendship with these

farmland owners with separate talks that lead up to how family of Laura and Phyllis

could help the other. Laura and Phyllis would thereafter tell their families about the

suggestion given to them."

"Shelly, I've got the picture. Thanks for everything. This is my first bad

experience as a benefactor. I want to continue to help people but now more careful about

trust. I will do my part for Linda in a matriarch role how things are or continue in her life

for possible use."

Paul was in the kitchen and there were no other customers in the eatery when

Linda served Victor his snack and they chatted with each other. Linda proudly told Victor

that the business made her and Paul wealthy enough to purchase the tenement building in

which their business was on the ground level and their apartment home above it. They

also bought the six-family tenement building to the left and the six-family tenement

building to the right of the building with their business and home---all of which increased their wealth.

Victor viewed this as a good time to suggested Linda become matriarch of her family group. She asked how to do it, and what the duties would be, if she could make rules to follow with punishment for who strays from the rules or The Family.

Victor never had a matriarch nor knew any family with a matriarch. His responses were what the average adult refused to accept from blood family and/or socially connected people. It included, "You offer yourself as matriarch, answer whatever questions they ask about you in that role, and wait for their unanimous acceptance of you as matriarch. Your greater wealth than theirs would inspire them to trust your guidance. Money is power. Money buys everything for even people who are unattractive and unappealing to other people. Money buys people from all walks of life if you know their wants, needs, and price tags. If you have unmarried adult family, you become a matchmaker for each to have a marriage mate. You encourage married couples to produce many children for the growth as one big family. You fix rules about when, where, and how often all would gather as a family. Your rules could follow the Catholic Church that uses different punishment for who strays from its laws."

"Victor, I like your idea. I'd like to be who they all honor and respect."

Linda appointed herself matriarch and was unanimously accepted by who she called family. None faulted her rules that included, "All must tell me everything said, done and talked about among yourselves and anyone with whom you connect. I must be told when someone new enters your lives, what type of relationship it is, and where it feels headed. Marriages help the growth of our combined families. I would be matchmaker for our unmarried adults. We follow Church rules about no divorce; who breaks a marriage must suffer many things. Marriages must produce children for continued growth of The Family. Our family further grows with family of who marries into our family. Punishments are also arranged for who would stray from the fold, and for who would refuse to pay a debt of any type or kind. We gather for weddings, anniversaries, births, birthdays, baptisms, and all holidays that require close of business doors to the public. In good weather, we'd gather for picnics in a nearby park where our growing children could run and play. Our womenfolk would bring food and drink for all to share in the park. On rainy days and cold weather, gatherings would in the home of Paul and I above the restaurant. Our restaurant supplies would be used, and our womenfolk would prepare and serve what is available and offered for all to enjoy."

Linda's list of family gatherings omitted school graduations during this time that she put no value to formal schooling. However, Linda believed that her role as matriarch permitted her to change and add rules to fit wants and needs for self and her children--- and she often did this.

More Work with Free Will

Anna and Barbara were new customers for the separate farmlands of Laura and Phyllis. These women became friends of each other in short time. Anna and Barbara separately suggested to Laura and Phyllis how their families could help each other. Laura and Phyllis told each other what their new friends suggested. Both agreed that the suggestion could benefit their separated families and would present it in a gathering of their family group.

Phyllis, Susan and Doctor Andrew met with each other to discuss whether to allow or not allow unrelated people to provide for Donald's family with five growing children. All agreed it would be a saving face way to free them of this duty to *take care of their own*. Doctor Andrew said, "Although I agree, I would never withhold medical care for my sister and her five growing children. Aside from that, we must decide how to deal with possibilities that who provides for Donald's family would seek returns that could be interpreted as buying and selling humans which is illegal in this country."

All agreed that who wanted this responsibility should make the offer directly to Donald and Patricia. And that any repayment for it should also be with only Donald and Patricia.

On Sunday, Linda and Paul made their weekly trip to the farmland for food items.

When at Laura's land, Laura told Linda: "My neighbor Phyllis has a brother whose drinking and gambling debts keep him from properly providing for his wife and five growing children. Their families have helped them in a variety of ways for the past thirteen years and see no good or right way to end it. The Bible says we are to help our countrymen; this is our chance to do it."

Linda said, "We could help but I must figure out what could be our returns for doing it. Get pictures of the five children and the current age of each child. The children could be marriage mates for our family group when older. I'll find out what this state's laws are for the youngest age that children could marry."

Linda was overjoyed when Laura gave her pictures of the children and their current ages. The oldest was thirteen-year-old Jean; next was eleven-year-old Rocco, followed by nine-year-old Sarah, seven-year-old Caesar, and three-year-old Lucy.

Linda said, "These are good looking children. When married into our families, children they produce would change the looks and shapes of our next generation. Their extended family with doctors and schoolteachers would help our families to climb social ladders. This state's law allows girls to marry when fourteen years old with parental consent. We follow the Bible's words to help our countrymen. In this situation, arrangements would benefit all with the union. The first marriage wouldn't take long after we get in the picture. Laura, you ask Phyllis if her family group would allow our families to replace them for their needy family of seven people. Tell her that our expected returns would be for the growing children to marry into our families when legally old enough to do so with parental consent."

Laura later telephoned Linda with encouraging news: "Phyllis gave me a piece of paper with the address of Donald's family unit, plus where he spends time gambling and drinking. Phyllis said none of her family could take away the rights of Donald and wife Patricia to accept or reject what is offered and wanted as returns. It means one of our family presents things to them, and another of us goes as witness to the offer and responses of Donald and his wife. You learned the marriage laws of this state, but we cannot ignore that the plans could be interpreted as buying and selling humans that is illegal in this country. Should we risk that arrangements must be done on an honor and trust basis?"

"Yes, we could handle things with trust. People of their high quality would not risk any shame if all doesn't go right." Linda chose Michael to connect with Donald where he drank and gambled. The connection brought an invitation for Michael and sister Laura to visit Donald and Patricia in their home. Parents sent their four older children outdoors to play but kept their three-year-old daughter Lucy by her mother. Patricia lived with the customs that only the husband makes family life decisions. Donald agreed that the offer to provide all needed for his family would better their lives now and would better his children's lives when old enough to marry.

During this meeting, Donald told Michael and Laura about his barber shop co-worker whose marriage produced six sons and two daughters. "He and his wife find it nearly impossible to provide well for their family of ten people on his barber wages. Their eight children and our five children are close in age; they are in different schools but spend much time together as if they were blood cousins. They enjoy each other's company at different occasions: family weddings, births, anniversaries, birthdays, school graduations, this country's holidays, and go to church together. The father of this family is a hardworking man. He isn't a heavy drinker and doesn't gamble. He wants to start a barber shop with a few workers on hand. He's a proud man but would take help as a loan and repay it with scheduled repayments."

Michael said, "We could talk with you and your co-worker about it after we talk with our family matriarch." When Michael and Laura were back with family, they told Linda about Donald's co-worker. Linda was overjoyed to have more children as future marriage partners for their family group. Linda didn't yet have pictures of these other children, but she believed they would be as good-looking as Donald's children. She called for a family meeting to discuss help for the family of ten people. Linda said, "The start of a barber shop wouldn't involve years of our help. Instead of a loan on a payment schedule, we would offer help with a promise that one or more of their children would marry into our families with parental consent when old enough. Our help to Donald's family of seven people would go on for years after the first growing girl is married into our families. It would be eleven years before their three-year-old girl could marry." All of Linda's family group agreed to be part of financial help to both struggling families.

Linda added, "More future grooms mean Bertha and I must deliver more daughters. More marriages mean more children for our growth as one big family. Michael, your next step is to collect the recorded legal names and birth dates of the five growing children and their parents. While we provide for them, they'll be listed on our yearly tax returns as charity dependents. When a girl is married into our families, she becomes the dependent of only her husband for his tax papers. On top of all else, these marriages make the separate families of Donald and Patricia become extended family for us."

Michael asked, "How do we know who marries who and when?"

Linda said, "No problem! Age will decide it for both sides. We would use the rules of England's Royalty who start with the eldest for their throne. Michael is the unmarried oldest among us. His bride will be the first girl, Jean who turns fourteen years old a few months before his twenty-eighth birthday. Their wedding would become Michael's birthday gift. Four years later, Jean's first sister Sarah turns fourteen years old and she becomes the bride for Lance, our next oldest unmarried one. Next in line for marriage would be my first son Chester; his bride would be Lucy who turns seventeen years old in the same year he turns eighteen years old and ready to marry as a responsible adult. A bride for my second son, Gino would be from the family with eight children. Michael and Lance would have beautiful brides much younger than they are. My sons would also have beautiful brides but closer to their own ages. Daughters of my cousin Bertha and Wayne would also marry based on age: Leslie the eldest and Jean's first brother Rocco would both turn eighteen years old in the year when they are to marry each other. Leslie's younger sister Paula would marry Rocco's younger brother Caesar when he turns eighteen years old and two years older than Paula. Bertha and I hope to produce more children with prayers they are daughters for the extra grooms from the family with eight children. The school system allows children to quit school when fourteen years old when needed by their family. I plan to use this rule for my sons to quit school when fourteen years old to make them paid employees in our family business. It would make my two sons be responsible men ready to marry and provide for a wife when eighteen years old."

Lance asked, "What happens to our widowed mother after Michael and I are married?"

Linda said, "Lance, as the last to marry you'd have the parent duty until your wedding day. Your bride would take and share your parent duty as a wedding package. Another way would be that on your wedding day, parent duty would pass to the married eldest son, Wayne and Bertha, who would have had the most time to adjust to married life and to parenthood."

Michael and Lance anxiously and simultaneously asked Linda the same question, "What happens from now to the first wedding among us?"

"We would get the future marriage partners and their parents accustomed to our different looks, shapes and ways as happens in schools where all type and kind of children are mixed with each other. We would invite them all to join us for every occasion that brings us together, with the addition of celebrating their special times. The family gatherings would let us see and touch some of what our money makes possible for them. We would have gifts for them as we now do among ourselves. Time would convince them that we are generous people who want them to be happy permanent parts of our lives."

Arranged Marriages Begin

Jean was a beautiful teenaged girl, five feet two inches tall with a well-proportioned figure, black wavy hair and hazel colored eyes. From a very young age, Jean missed much formal schooling to help mother during pregnancy, to help raise her four younger siblings and helped with her mother's wage paid sewing work at home.

Jean refused talk about her becoming a bride. "My mother needs me to help raise my sisters and younger brothers. She needs me to help her with the sewing work we do at home for the money we need."

Doctor Andrew said nothing to his niece Jean and didn't interfere with how Donald's two sisters handled the situation. Patricia sat quietly nearby as her husband's sister Phyllis told Jean, "Your mother worries about the future for all her children. If you married the wealthy bachelor, your mother would be happy about you are being well provided for; she would see this as rewards for how much you've done to help her in in many ways throughout the years."

Patricia remained silent as Donald's sister Susan told Jean, "Your mother's concerns about money for clothes and footwear with each child's growth would be less if you were married with your husband having duty to provide these things for you. Marriage would also provide you with a better life than you've had. The rich bachelor could buy you fur coats and jewelry that would make you feel like a different and happy person."

Linda expected Jean's extended family to make her ready to marry. At a gathering of Linda's family group, she announced her plans: "Michael's gift of a bride will be on his twenty-eighth birthday. Their wedding guests must include the doctors, nurses, and teachers that are part of his bride's family; guests will also include who connects with them. Michael has the wealth to cut no corners to make it a lavish wedding to impress all who attend, to make some jealous, and get the attention of our local newspaper. Their wedding should give belief to others who marry into our families that they would be given nothing less lavish. Michael would pay for his bride's choice of clothes, clothes for her parents, clothes for his own mother, and for all the bridal party. He would pay the costs of flowers for the church, for his bride, for the bridal party and for his bride's parents. He pays for vehicles that take the bride, bridal party and bride's parents to the church, for vehicles that take all from the church to the reception where all are served plenty of good food and drinks."

Neighbors and friends of Jean's family were invited and attended her wedding. Among them were Robert, his brother Rudy and their widowed mother Celeste. As Linda and Bertha roamed about in the reception hall, they heard Robert tell his mother about his dream to be a doctor. Linda approached him and said, "My cousin Bertha and I overheard your talk about a dream to be a doctor. We could help to make it come true for you."

Robert asked, "How?"

"With arrangements for you to marry a woman with rich parents who would pay all costs for you to become a doctor after the wedding. The bride in mind is Stella who is years older than you. Wedding plans could be made for when you turn eighteen years old and have graduated high school. If this is what you want, it won't take much time and effort to arrange it." Linda pointed to where Stella and her parents were seated alone at a small table. "From here, you could see Stella and her parents before you decide."

Linda and Robert saw the nod of "yes" from his mother and he accepted Linda's offer. Linda was satisfied that it held no pressure and had advance approval of Robert's mother. The next step was for Linda and Bertha to secure the approval of Stella and her parents who were as anxious as Stella for her to marry. Stella looked to where Linda pointed to see Robert seated with his brother and their mother alone at a small table. Linda presented Stella with high points if she and Robert married each other: "A groom younger than yourself would be feathers in your cap. When he is a licensed doctor with a private practice it would make people more jealous of you. A doctor in the family would be something for your parents to also boast about." Stella and her parents agreed to the union.

* * * * * * * * * * * * *

Sarah was a thirteen-year-old aunt when the marriage of her sister Jean and Michael produced their first child who was named Lewis. Lewis was born three weeks before Christmas. Sarah was to be the bride of Michael's younger brother Lance when she turned fourteenth years old five months from now. Sarah had good looks, dark brown wavy hair, and brown eyes. She was slightly overweight for her five feet four-inch height.

Lewis was less than a year old when Linda insisted that Michael and Jean immediately employ a governess for this child and other children their marriage produced. She told Michael, "Having a governess would be another good thing for Jean's sisters to look forward to when married into our families."

The wedding for Sarah and Lance was discussed at a gathering to celebrate Lewis' birth and his first Christmas. She refused to honor the arrangements made when she was nine years old. Her soft voice became loud as she said, "No one could speak on behalf of another person. We are people with feelings. Our clothes shouldn't be touched and felt as if fabric bought to make hats or clothes. Parent duty shouldn't be a wedding package. Starting marriage with a third party wouldn't give the couple time to adjust to each other or adjust to being married. Also, I don't want to marry anyone who isn't my equal with good looks and class quality. The good of our ancestors resulted in a city with our family name in Italy and on maps of Italy. Our family is educated, intelligent people who contribute to the world in different ways. What good things could any of your family group say about your lives?"

Based on Linda's rules, Sarah's rejection of Lance made her younger sister Lucy next in line to be his bride. Linda and Lance battled with each other about who was entitled to Lucy: Was Lucy to be Lance's bride or remain the bride for Linda's son Chester as was originally arranged?

Lucy angrily interrupted this battle: "It's horrifying to be fought over as if a girl had no rights or a say about her life. It's worse to be fought over by ugly and evil people. Your kind made a bride of a child. You're the marketplace for ugly people yet rejected by your own kind. Lincoln freed slaves a long time ago and bondage is against the law in America. No one could speak on behalf of other people. Not even parents could make their children forever responsible for their debts. People are polite to show tolerance for whom and what is different, but no one should be forced to like or want someone as a friend or for marriage."

Linda responded to only one part of Lucy's words: "Your families let a child become a bride. How does that make your family better than us?"

Lucy ignored Linda's words and continued to talk: "Opposites of so much shouldn't be mixed. The Bible says that *no one can stand against jealousy*. Egos of ugly people blow up with pride when seen with their opposites. Girls with good looks and good shapes who are seen with an ugly man are viewed as Gold Diggers or desperate to marry. People are judged by whom they are seen with. Looks are important because it's the first thing seen in the morning and last thing seen when lights are closed for the night. The quality of people who are extreme opposites matters when married to each other. Opposites of so much don't understand each other. Your type pulls people down to gutter levels because change is too much for any of you. Your type exhaust polite excuses and good manners until it results in lost patience, lost self-control, and crude ways and words to match yours.

"You boast about how much wealth you have but there's no proof of it with how you all dress for the public, including face make-up and hairdo for your womenfolk. Nothing about your lives is personal or sacred. Personal issues are discussed with your customers. You punish your children in the presence of customers. Your business employees are only your family. All things about your type are embarrassments and insults for people of good quality and class. Couples don't marry only each other. They become part of each other's family. The wrong marriage decision of one family part would split or destroy that person's family."

Linda responded with short sentences to only parts of Lucy's words: "People close their eyes to kiss, and don't see the looks of who they kiss. Food and liquid spills ruin clothes in our work. Strangers can't always be trusted to work in a family business."

Bertha also responded to only one part of Lucy's words: "Reasons to punish a child are forgotten if not done when needed."

Bertha's nine-year-old daughter Nancy interrupted for her contribution to all said here: "People can't help how they are born or how they grow. We could learn new and different ways to live, behave, and dress, but it's not taught in our schools. Our ability to learn has been proven with the high school marks of my two older sisters. We work hard for the money we have; this gives us the right to expect returns for what we give or do. It's a dog-eat-dog life."

Lucy responded, "Nothing proves that all of you want to change. Linda kept her sons from school when only fourteen years old to help in the diner's kitchen. Both sons lack social graces in addition to being cheated of a good and proper education. Wives don't want to spend marriage as a teacher or mother to a husband who is supposed to be a grown and responsible man. The partner being taught new and different life ways often ends up feeling put down and grows to resentment that destroys their marriage. People who boast they have money for more than one lifetime hire people to run their business and for its book work. They have homes in different country parts and different parts of the world; they have expensive cars with chauffeurs and time to enjoy life. People who want to better their lives would do more with their business. The diner could be made into a high-class, full-service restaurant. Bertha and Wayne could make their tavern into a high-class cocktail lounge that served food."

Linda again interrupted Lucy: "Women who don't contribute to marriage offer only good looks and a nice shape. Money to provide well is all that matters. It makes no sense to give up a successful business for an unpredictable future. Money is saved for life's Golden Years, and to help children starts with marriage. Some people need help to remember money is needed for the basic needs of food, clothes, shelter, and warm home in the winter. Life gives chances for people with big ideas to prove themselves or *eat their words and ways*."

Rocco and Caesar were brothers of Jean, Sarah and Lucy. Rocco grew to be six feet tall, had good looks and a firm body. His voice was stronger than usual when he gave his opinions. Caesar grew to only five feet five inches, had good looks, a firm body but softer voice when he expressed his strong opinions without yelling. Allen, their adopted cousin was small boned with a slightly thin body for his five feet four-inch height; his voice squeaked as he also gave his strong opinions. Rocco, Caesar and Allen added to what each said at different times:

"No one refuses freely given money."

"People who gamble on the future take the risks of losing like all other gamblers."

"We don't want to marry girls who look like men or look and act like a monkey."

"We don't want to rock the cradle."

"We don't want size differences for Mutt and Jeff or Laurel and Hardy jokes."

"We don't want a wife who was spoiled and pampered before her wedding."

"We don't want to feel like kept men, gigolos, or puppets on the purse strings of a wife and her family."

"Take your ideas and shove them up your ...."

Linda interrupted with a raised hand as she said, "Wait and rethink. Everyone knows that nothing is for free. Not even welfare money is given without a proven need."

After then, relationships quickly changed. Linda confessed to feeling *jealous and left out* of the close bonds that grew for Bertha and Jean as they worked together in the business of their husbands. Linda worked Lance to view Jean as a constant reminder of being rejected for marriage by her sister Sarah. About when Lance broke from the business partnership, Linda convinced Wayne and Michael that neither could add Lance's shopping duties to their work for the business. Bertha and Wayne soon agreed to also sell their partnership shares to Michael.

Jean agreed with Michael's decision to buy partnership shares from his brothers. At a meeting, Michael told Lance, Wayne and Bertha, "My wife and I feel we could independently keep the business profitable with longer hours in it and longer hours for our children's governess. I would make trips to the to buy needed items along with my work to mold hats; Jean would cut the fabric to be molded along with her work to finish each hat. We'd pay a boy who is old enough boy to deliver items to retail shop owners as Lance did." Michael accepted the payment schedule that Wayne and Lance made for him to buy out their partnership shares.

Wayne and Bertha began a tavern business. They bought the building in which the tavern was on ground level and their apartment home above it. They also bought the tenancy building next to it with a narrow alley that separated these two buildings.

Lance became involved with refilling candy and cigarettes in vending machines --- with changing recorded music in juke boxes --- with checks on the condition of pinball machines --- and collected money from each machine. This work put him in different parts of the city and introduced him to new people. To occupy time alone with his

widowed mother, Lance learned to forge birth certificates and other documents for who

needed it for whatever reason or purpose; this work increased the number of new people

in his life.

Linda Regains Power

Months after the Christmas Day battles about marriages, the families gathered in a nearby public park for Memorial Day. Jean's siblings, parents and extended family were part of it. All were seated near to each other when Linda stood with a raised hand and a strong voice: "Representatives of the tax bureau recently told my husband and me that it's against the law to list people as dependents that didn't live with us, and that ignorance of the law was no excuse. We were fined big penalties with interest for the eleven years we weren't entitled to do it. The same thing happened for Bertha and Wayne, and for Lance. We don't expect anyone to admit having made this happen, but we can add two plus two. The tax auditors gave us copies of their paperwork in this matter. It is our proof of how many years we provided for the family of seven people. These proofs also help belief that the families of Donald and Patricia *used* us.

"We can be just as spiteful. With or without these proofs, anyone can be bought for whatever purpose. Our customers are public transportation drivers, people who use it, and nearby business owners and their employees. Customers at the tavern of Bertha and Wayne are people who go there to use the billiard tables, for juke box music they listen or dance to, some go there after the movie theater, after they leave a dance hall, and some families go for a meal together. Anyone can be bought if you know their price tag. But there is also the power of gossip that becomes believable when something is repeated by more than one person or group of people."

As Linda spoke, Nina heard Aunt Lucy mumble, "No one knows if something would boomerang."

Seven-year-old Nina asked Aunt Lucy, "What do you mean boomerang?"

Aunt Lucy replied, "I just thought aloud of a boomerang as a toy for people of all ages."

Nina also heard her father's mumbled word: "Benefactor punishment is pushed to the back burner. She becomes the winner again!"

Nina spoke to her father, "Family talk to themselves a lot with words I know but not how family use the words. What did you mean about punishment? Whose punishment and for what?

Michael replied, "It's adult matters. It shouldn't involve your generation. It shouldn't!"

Lance with Parent Duty

Lance remembered Linda's rule that marriage duty passed to the next younger one

when the arranged one rejected it---and that Linda refused to follow her rule was to make

Lucy replace Sarah as his bride. Lance also remembered that Linda said parent duty

would pass to Wayne and Bertha on his wedding day, but they refused to take the duty.

He asked Wayne and Bertha to make tenants of him and mother for them to check on her

while he was at work and searched for a bride; they again refused:

"We have long hours in our tavern. We prepare and serve food for lunch onward

into nighttime closing. Our growing daughters need our time and attention. We're left

with very little time to rest that leaves no time to care for an aging parent. Our elderly

tenants have lived here for very many years. We couldn't evict them knowing they have

no other place. You and mother now have a nice place to live that's close to a big

shopping area. Someday you'll find a bride who would take your parent duty as a

wedding package. Parent duty is part of life for many families and continues to be part of

some weddings."

Lance believed he could rent a room and live alone if Michael took duty of their

mother. Michael and Jean didn't own property and didn't use their rented apartment's

living room for company. Most of their time, six days a week was in their ground level business and the big kitchen behind it. Their rented apartment is where their governess, Emma cared for their children who were not yet school age, cared for their older children when ill, with added duties that included housekeeping and laundry.

Michael apologetically told Lance, "We have four children and another child on the way. We could possibly convert our apartment living room into a bedroom, but it doesn't seem to be the best answer for your situation. It wouldn't be right to expect our mother to climb to and from our third-floor apartment. Our governess is with us for only daytime hours Monday through Friday. On Saturdays Jean and I have our children with us in the large kitchen behind our business with Sundays our only time to bond as a family. We are just unable to help you."

Lance sought help from Linda and Paul who owned three tenancy buildings They refused to make tenants of Lance and mother. Linda said, "We are not blood related and I don't have a duty to help with your parent duty. Your situation is a family matter that must be settled with your brothers and sister."

Lance's only sister lived on her farm far from where he and brothers lived. Lance didn't seek his sister's help because he knew his mother wanted to be near to where her sons lived. Lance and his mother moved into an apartment building that was mostly occupied by elderly people. The elderly residents checked on each other and helped each other whenever possible. However, this did not relieve or ease the bitterness and grudges Lance held against his family.

A Bride for Lance

The death of Lance's widowed mother freed him for marriage. He continued to be a bachelor of good means, who could provide well. However, he felt that being in his mid-thirties was too old to marry and too old to start a family of his own. He remained embittered with a badly bruised ego.

Lucy's brother Rocco understood that their troubled family life would continue if Lance remained unmarried. Rocco visited his sister Jean where he collected updated pictures and information about Michael's family group. Rocco was determined to find a bride for Lance with hopes it would soften Lance's hurt feelings and free Lucy for Linda's son Chester. Rocco ignored Lucy's resentment that her two brothers could refuse duty marriages for a bride of their choice, while she could not. Lucy felt this way while she also understood that sons passed the family name to sons. She knew that children produced with a good-looking spouse made them fit with the families they were born into. Lucy knew that Linda wanted opposites as marriage mates for her offspring to produce children with good-looks and nice shapes to change their next generation as it did with children produced in the marriage of Michael and Jean.

Rocco's fiancée, Ella lived with her family in a different part of the big city from where Rocco lived with his younger siblings and parents. He joined Ella for Sunday services in the church she regularly attended. It was the church where parishioners included a troubled family of seven adult siblings. In one Mass, Rocco heard the priest call for special prayers *to help the family of seven regain a peaceful life*. After Mass, parishioners gathered in front of the church. Rocco overheard their talk about a family of seven siblings. Ella stayed silent as she followed Rocco to that group where he asked if any of them knew why there were special prayers in today's Mass and if any of them knew the family it was for. One of the women pointed to where a woman stood with two priests as she said, "Those two priests are with their unmarried sister Julie. She passed the normal age to marry and produce children but is still anxious for a groom. Those three people are part of seven brothers and sisters who continued to be a family after both parents passed away."

Rocco asked, "How do you know so much about this family?"

"We live a few houses from each other. It's in an area where neighbors become friends but it's more like one big family."

Rocco asked, "Why the special prayer for them to regain a peaceful life?"

"The family couldn't make a brother end his adulterous behavior to avoid divorce. They are part of our group of families that disapprove of divorce and it has hurt Julie's chance for a suitable groom. Troubled life worsened for them when the divorced brother and his mistress ran away without concern for the financial needs of his ex-wife, Millie and their three growing young children in her custody.

Rocco began to believe that fixing Julie and Lance for marriage would help them have the married life they wanted. He believed that Julie would fit well into Lance's family group without jealousy issues: Julie was a short overweight woman with a big nose, small eyes and thin lips. If Julie and Lance married each other, the only family debt of parents was for Lucy to marry Chester. After next Sunday's Mass, Rocco and Ella approached Julie who stood alone in front of the church and searched her purse for whatever. Rocco approached Julie. "Hello. My name is Rocco. This is my fiancée, Ella. We could take you home in my car if you're not waiting for someone else to do it."

"Thank you for the offer. I'm not expecting anyone. This is where I wait for the bus that gets me home after Sunday Mass. I've seen you two together in church before today. It's nice to have a chance to meet both of you."

Rocco said, "You appear troubled. If you want to talk about it, Ella and I would take you for coffee and a snack in a quiet corner of a nearby restaurant. We could take you home after that."

Julie was hungry for people to talk to about her troubled life---people who may have new ideas that might help her. She omitted talk about her divorced brother's second wife whose brother was lawyer Benji. Julie didn't say that lawyer Benji helped her divorced brother and second wife run away together with new birth certificates that dropped the last letter of his family name. Nor did Julie say she knew the whereabouts of this runaway couple. Julie's talk concentrated on her brother's divorce and that it heavily shamed her family. She talked about her two brothers who are priests and gossip about them not having corrected their brother's adulterous ways to prevent his divorce. With continued talks, Rocco learned the movie theater that Julie visited every Saturday afternoon. It worked well with information that Lance worked in this theater's lobby on Saturdays. About one hour before the film began, Lance refilled candy and cigarette vending machines for weekend customers and collected money from these vending machines.

After next Sunday's church services, Rocco, Ella and Julie again went for coffee and a snack in the same restaurant. Rocco told Julie about Lance: "He is part of families that my older sister married into. He was the last home with his widowed mother but couldn't find a bride willing to share his parent duty when married. His ego suffered with rejection for marriage. His mother recently passed, and he is now free to marry. He is a man of good means who could provide very well. He needs a woman who could build his ego and make him feel that being in his mid-thirties is not too old to marry and start a family. This is a recent picture of Lance. If you are interested in him for marriage, I could help the two of you to connect with each other without it looking or feeling like it was an arrangement."

Julie responded, "The picture makes him look like a decent person. His ability to provide well helps to make him a suitable husband"

Rocco told Julie what day and time of day Lance was in the movie theater that she went to on Saturdays. The next Saturday, Julie was first in line for her theater ticket, after which she sat in its lobby where cigarette and candy vending machines stood. While Lance refilled the machines, Julie looked at the picture of him in her purse and then closed her purse. She went to the vending machine where Lance was at work. Julie spoke to Lance as he refilled the candy machine. "Hello Mr. Good-Looking. Do you plan to fill this machine with my favorite candy?"

They chatted with each other about thirty minutes while Lance did his work at a slow pace. There was only about five minutes before the film was to begin when Julie said, "I come to this theater alone every Saturday at the same time. I buy my ticket about an hour before the film begins and sit in the lobby until the film showing starts. Would I see you here every Saturday about this time of day?”

“Yes, I come here every Saturday about the same time to refill these vending machines and collect money from each machine.”

“Next Saturday I could miss the movie for you and me to spend time to get to know each other in a nearby restaurant.”

“It sounds good to me. I’ll rearrange next Saturday’s work schedule.”

It was a short courting stage for Julie and Lance. Julie told Lance the problems of her family. Lance didn’t tell her that he forged a new birth certificate for her divorced brother. Lance offered a way to relieve troubled life for her family. Julie agreed with private presentation of his plan to his family group at the wedding reception before their other guests arrived.

Wedding of Lance and Julie

Lance paid all costs for his wedding that included clothes for the bride, flowers for the church, and transportation for all. With reservations for transportation, he arranged that only his family group and Julie's siblings be the first taken to the reception location. Other guests were to be taken there thirty minutes after that. Lance was thirty-five years old and Julie was twenty-eight years old when wed to each other. Their expensive wedding with many guests did not draw the attention of the local newspaper as happened with the wedding of Michael and Jean.

Julie's siblings and their extended family were guests at her wedding. However, their divorced brother's ex-wife, Millie and her three growing children were not invited to it.

Julie was seated with her siblings and Lance's family when he stood in front of them all. He knew that what he was to announce would surprise them all: "Thirteen years ago, Linda was our newly appointed family matriarch who used the Bible's instructions for us to *help thy countrymen.* Eleven years of our funds provided for a family with five growing children with whom we had no blood ties. Our agreed to returns were for those children to marry into our family group when old enough to marry but these promised repayments didn't happen.

"Julie is now part of my family and I am part of her family. The troubled life of Julie's family worsened when her divorced brother ran away and hasn't been found to comply with the court order for alimony and child support. The ex-wife's gossip blamed Julie's priest brothers for not having successfully corrected their brother's behavior before divorced. I now use the Bible's words *to help thy countrymen.* Julie and I believe her brother's ex-wife Millie would be calmed if her growing children were arranged with marriage mates to better their lives. My family group have successful businesses to make this happen.

"I've arranged the following marriage partners for our growing children to marry Millie's growing children, two sons and one daughter. I have pictures of these children for our family's children to know who is to be their marriage mate.

"Millie's eldest child Rick and Linda's only daughter Lynn will marry each other. ______ Linda's sons would be like older brothers for Rick and help him become part of their family diner business. Lewis, the first son of Michael and Jean will marry Millie's only daughter, Carmella. If Lewis refused, his duty would pass to his two younger brothers with Linda's rules about duty passing. Also, with Linda's duty passing rules, one of Wayne and Bertha's the eldest of their three daughters will marry Millie's second son Carlos and make him part of their tavern business. There are no blood tie issues with these marriages. Although Millie and her children are not guests at this wedding, she has advance information about these arranged marriages. Our families have witnessed punishment for who has refused a duty marriage. Millie and her children have experienced punishments with divorce. These examples help for all of these marriages to be carried out as arranged without divorce."

Lance's family group made no facial or physical expression to indicate their feelings. Nor did any of them openly comment about these arranged marriages. Thirty minutes passed. Their wedding guests were now entering the reception hall. Bride, groom and bridal party now took their assigned seats. During breaks from provided music, Michael played his accordion; his two daughters sang the words to the music and each girl improvised dance steps to it. Linda's children did not sing or dance. Wayne and Bertha's youngest daughter Nancy did not sing or dance. Nancy's two older sisters had musical talents but enjoyed listening to Michael's accordion and watching the talent of his daughters. Linda three offspring had no musical talents; after she listened to and watched Michael's daughters, Linda's firm voice unexpectedly said, "Not everyone has God given talents of any kind."

Michael had one too many alcoholic drinks when he openly said, "I have the youngest and most beautiful bride of my family and gave me the most beautiful children of them all." He didn't see the reactions of the newlywed and his family group who then silently viewed him as a braggart. (A decade later, Michael understood this but could no longer change the consequences that were arranged for him, his wife and their children.)

Divorced Millie and Children

Millie knew that divorce was unacceptable to the families and to their church, but she couldn't foresee how it would severely change life for self and her growing children. When Millie faced the consequences, she refused to blame it on her decision to divorce. She taught her children who to blame for what she and they suffered until they believed it. She made her children believe that families of their runaway father and new wife *owed* for their hurt lives---owed for having punished her divorce---that punishment added injury to insult when none found their father to enforce the court ordered money they needed. This was Millie's priority instead work for her children to become responsible adults. Like Linda, but for different reasons, Millie wasn't concerned about her children's formal education to better their lives. All that mattered was payment for their hurt and troubled lives.

Millie had black wavy hair, brown eyes, large nose, full size lips and overweight for her five feet two-inch height. She was employed as a seamstress in a sewing factory where she talked to them and whoever else listened about her divorce from a womanizing husband: "Two of his brothers are priests, but they didn't make him end cheating behavior. The wife of my ex-husband has a brother who is a lawyer, but lawyer Benji didn't prove he helped to find the runaway couple to enforce the court order for alimony and child support. Loss of needed funds added injury to insult. I know these families arranged our troubled life because I know it's some of the ways they use to punish people for different reasons. Deducting union dues from my wages, in addition to federal and state taxes, lessened what's needed to support my family. Families of my ex-husband and his new wife have shown no concern for my growing children. I know my gossip about those families hurts their lives, but I won't stop it until someone, or something has paid for the hurt lives arranged for my children and me.

"My children needed me home as a full-time mother, but the situation forced me to be employed. It meant my children are alone after school until my workday end. My greatest worry has been the youngest child, Carlos. He was ready for school when his parents were divorced. He behaved the worst since his father disappeared. I refused to believe people who said Carlos would outgrow bad behavior and I figured out a way to not worry about him: Taxes from my earnings are part of wages for workers in the court system who didn't find my ex-husband to enforce the court order. Taxes from my earnings are also part of salaries for employees in the school system. Schoolteachers become my babysitters. With Carlos' start in kindergarten, I told him we'd share a secret for him to be bad in any way that made a teacher detain him. This way I didn't have to worry about him, and he wouldn't be alone before I was back home."

Millie's plan worked but, Carlos' bad behavior wasn't only inside the classroom. It was unacceptable on school grounds where children waited for the bell to be in class. It was also not acceptable behavior for lunch breaks when many children ate packed lunch in the school's outdoor grounds. Bad behavior made Carlos friendless. Children of Michael and Jean and the children of Millie attended the same school. Gossip helped

Carlos to know that he and Lewis became cousins after his aunt Julie and Lewis' uncle Lance married each other. While on school grounds, Carlos ran after Lewis, and Lewis attempted to avoid Carlos.

Lewis followed Linda's rule to tell her about everyone in life, including where and how it would go. Linda was now more concerned about life for her family---for her two sons, daughter and their restaurant business. She remembered that Michael's wife Jean had a paternal aunt Vanessa who was a schoolteacher with seniority in the school attended by Millie's children and children of Michael and Jean. Millie's eldest child, Rick was to graduate elementary school in three months; Vanessa was the only English teacher for eighth grade students. Linda used the tax audit proofs to use Vanessa to free her family of duty with Rick. Linda was determined for her children to have marriage mates that would afford social climbs; and for their marriages to produce their next generation with good looks and nice shapes to also change their visual images. Linda wanted returns for her eleven years of spent money after freed of duty with Rick in ways that left her with *clean hands*.

Fourteen-year-old Rick delivered newspapers after school while his mother was at work, and on weekends when she believed he was with friends. He saved earnings and tips for social time with friends he expected to make when in high school.

Linda used Lucy to have her Aunt Vanessa get help from other schoolteachers to encourage Rick to run away from home. Schoolteachers were careful to avoid legal charges of aiding and abetting the delinquency of a minor but could suggest he consult a priest for help with a foster home until he reached the legal age of 21 years. Rick's different teachers convinced him that he could make a better life for himself if he could break from siblings and mother. They made him believe the break would give him chances for a high school education to better his life. On the day Rick graduated grammar school, he wore more clothes than needed with plans to hitch hike out of the area to a southern state. He never returned to his mother and could never be found. Millie viewed Rick's run-away as another punishment for divorce.

Six Days Before Christmas

The yearly Thanksgiving Day family gathering was again held in the home of Linda and Paul. Wayne and Bertha attended with their three growing daughters. Michael and Jean attended with their five growing children. Lance and Julie did not attend. They could not forget their wedding day when Michael said he had the youngest and most beautiful bride of his family.

During this holiday gathering Michael and Jean's eight-year-old daughter Nina was ready to leave the bathroom when she heard the voices of Aunt Linda and Aunt Bertha. Nina was still behind the closed door when she clearly heard them plan to punish someone before the coming Christmas---about four weeks from now. Nina didn't hear them say the name of who was the *braggart* to be punished. When back to family, Nina pulled her father away from everyone and told him what she heard: "We'll take care of the braggart. His words hurt the joyous day it should have been for the bride and groom."

Michael didn't yet think about what he said at the wedding when he told Nina, "Forget what you think you heard. Their talk wasn't in front of the door for you to clearly understand all they said. It's possible that you misunderstood what was said."

Before the end of the Thanksgiving Day gathering, Bertha told Michael and his family, "Our family won't attend the party for Lewis' tenth birthday that Linda has planned. We want to do this in our home on the week before Christmas; this way Lewis won't think that our birthday gifts are only Christmas gifts. Jean should bring only Lewis to our home that day; full attention would be to only him. We chose a Sunday for this because your business and our business are closed to the public on Sundays. Jean's sister Lucy gave Linda and me her promise that she would be with you, Michael to help with your four younger children on that day. Lucy has plans to party with school friends that night, but she lives only around the corner from your place. She'd have enough time to get ready for the party after Jean and Lewis return home."

Michael saw Jean's nod of *yes* when he said, "It makes sense to make a special day before Christmas to celebrate Lewis' tenth birthday. I appreciate that you arranged help for me with our younger children. Also, your time for the party means Jean and Lewis would be back home before the regular bedtime for our children."

On the day of the of Lewis' birthday party, Michael, Jean, and their five children were in the big kitchen behind their business when Lucy arrived. Jean and Lewis quickly departure to the taxi that waited in front of the building. After Jean and Lewis left, Lucy and Michael sat at the kitchen table where both had a cup of freshly poured coffee. Sleeping sixteen-month-old chubby Jerry was his carriage. Nearly four-year-old Donald, nearly seven-year-old Tricia, and eight-year-old Nina were busy coloring books on the floor a good distance away from the hot coal burning stove that was used to heat this kitchen and to cook food.

Seventeen-year-old Lucy lost little time to remind Michael about her plans to be with friends that night. "The party is for my classmates and me to celebrate next week's

Christmas holiday before we must all be with only our families. I want to rest and not feel rushed to dress for this occasion. Jerry is asleep in his carriage and Donald is happy with what he's doing. Nina and Tricia are old enough to help without me in the picture. Nina and Tricia could be as helpful as their mother was from when eight years old and with siblings younger than herself: Nina could clear the kitchen table of leftover food and put it in the refrigerator. She could put the used plates, utensils and cookware in this sink where Tricia could wash all of it. Nina would dry and put away what was washed. Tricia must face the wall for duties at the sink, but Nina could keep watch of her brothers while doing her duties. And you are nearby to see that all goes well while you do the work for your business. Does it make sense? Do you agree?"

"Your idea makes sense. Go and enjoy time with your friends." Although surprised with this changed plan, Michael knew Lucy was always interested in only what mattered to her. As the youngest of five children and youngest of three girls, Lucy was always treated like a princess by two older brothers and expected the same treatment from everyone else.

Jean and Lewis arrived at the home of Wayne and Bertha at the scheduled time of day. Their nine-year-old daughter Nancy put the outdoor clothes of her Aunt Jean and cousin Lewis in the hall closet. Everyone sat quietly when tall and chubby Bertha announced, "As woman of the home, only I start this party and continue with it." All that Bertha said and did that day would stretch the time that Jean and Lewis were there. Plates, silverware, glasses and cups from the cupboard were slowly placed on the kitchen table as Bertha said who was to sit where.

Bertha refused to let anyone help her. Her slow-paced steps took the different

flavors of soda and then the cake from the refrigerator and put it all on the kitchen table.
She stood at her place at the table with hand motions for all to stand up and sing *Happy
Birthday* to Lewis. Bertha cut the cake and put a slice of it on the seven plates. She then
took ice cream from the freezer for a scoop of vanilla or chocolate on each slice of cake.
Bertha refilled the glasses with soda for the children and poured fresh coffee into cups for
the adults.

When finished in the kitchen, Bertha directed all to the living room where the
Happy Birthday song would be repeated with music by her two older daughters: Fifteen-
year-old Leslie played the piano and twelve-year-old Paula sang the words. Nancy had no
musical talents and carried out duties with birthday gifts. She slowly removed one gift at
a time from the foyer closet and put each in a corner of the dining room where Lewis
could see but not yet touch. Piano music and the birthday song ended when Nancy had all
gifts out of the closet. Bertha now gave Wayne a signal to be an open part of the party.
He was standing when he spoke to Lewis, "Tell us what you plan to do with life when
you are grown."

Lewis was too anxious to open his gifts and no one could make him say more
than one sentence about his future: "I don't know yet, but I want to do what makes me
feel important, what makes me wealthy and what makes everyone look up to me with
respect."

Bertha put an arm around Lewis' shoulders and said, "We want you to open each
gift here so we can see your reaction to each gift and your say thank you to each gift
giver. Tradition is for family's eldest offspring to be first in line; this time it will be the
opposite with Nancy the first with a gift to you." Lewis wasted no time unwrapping the

gifts---separate gifts with tags that showed the name of the gift. His *thank you* to each giver was short as he rushed to the next gift.

Jean interrupted: "If things continue this way, it would be past my children's normal bedtime before Lewis and I are back home."

Bertha's word included lies: "Our telephone isn't working for a call to call Michael to let him know you both would return home later than expected. A telephone repairman is due early tomorrow. But you needn't worry. Lucy promised to help Michael with the children until you and Lewis are back home."

Michael was concerned that Jean and Lewis weren't home yet and wondered why Bertha's telephone had a constant busy signal. He reheated refrigerated food for the children's supper and was concerned about their bedtime. He must still put more coal in the basement cellar furnace for heat to reach their third-floor apartment. Before he went down to the basement, he gave his daughters instructions that followed what Lucy suggested: "Nina, you put all leftover food into the refrigerator, clean the kitchen table, and put what must be washed into the kitchen sink. As Tricia washed those things, you dry what was cleaned and put it in their proper places.

"As done earlier today, Tricia would face the wall for her duty, so you keep watch of Donald who now plays with cleaned pots on the kitchen floor. You also watch for if Jerry wakes up and tries to get out of his carriage even though he hasn't learned to walk yet."

Michael found everyone and everything okay after his first trip to and from the basement. Jerry was still asleep in his carriage. Michael put a pot of water for coffee on the kitchen's hot coal stove. He relied on repeated reminders to the children to never touch or go near hot stoves, and that the children always obeyed the rule. He must check for how much heat reached their third-floor apartment and again risked leaving his children for another short time. He was anxious for a fresh cup of coffee. He put the coffee pot with clean fresh water on the hot stove and calculated that it would be ready for the coffee grinds when he returned.

It was December 19th---six days before Christmas. Nina continued to believe there was a Santa Clause who checked his lists for who was naughty or nice. Jerry remained asleep in his carriage; Donald still played with clean pots on the floor near to the sink where Tricia washed all in it. Nina decided to surprise her father with ready-made coffee when he returned. Tricia heard Nina drag a chair to the stove and saw her climb onto it to see if the water was ready for the coffee grinds. Tricia left sink duty and went to Nina's side that had the good eye vision. She made a strong pull on Nina's starched dress and as she said, "You know we're never to go near or touch hot stoves." And quickly returned to her duty at the sink.

These children were taught to look at who spoke to them and who they talked to. Nina was still on the chair at the stove when she turned to face Tricia who turned to hear Nina say, "I remember the warnings and I'm being extra careful while doing this."

As they faced each other, the part of Nina's dress that Tricia pulled down touched the hot stove and went aflame. Nina screamed and Donald began to cry. Tricia's hands went to her face with eyes filled with fright. Nina jumped off the chair and headed to the hallway as the flames more quickly took her dress. When Michael heard Nina yelling *Daddy! Daddy! Daddy!* he quickly met her on the second-floor landing where he removed his wool jacket to smother the flames. He carried her to the first-floor kitchen where the other children remained. He carefully removed Nina's clothes, used cold butter on her burned body parts, loosely wrapped her in a big towel and sat her on a chair by the kitchen table.

Michael telephoned for an ambulance. The ambulance quickly responded but emergency medical men couldn't provide the care Nina needed. Michael told the ambulance medics, "Childcare help didn't stay. My wife and first son haven't returned when expected. I used cold butter to cool my daughter's burned body."

The ambulance medics told Michael, "Butter worsened the burn injuries. Our records show service at this address, but the situation is extremely serious; we can't lose more time here. This child will be taken to the closest hospital from here---Saint Michael's Medical Center. Papers we leave with you show its location. She will be evaluated and cared for there with waits for one or both parents. We suggest that you telephone someone to help calm you and your other children."

After the ambulance left with Nina, Michael telephoned Linda and to tell her, "Lucy broke her promise to help. I always got a busy signal with calls to find out why Jean and Lewis weren't back when expected. My wool jacket stopped Nina's dress from burning more of her body. The ambulance took her to Saint Michael's Medical Center where they wait for Jean or me to get there." Michael didn't tell Linda why the accident happened, and Linda didn't ask. Although it was the time of day when the business of Linda and Paul was closed, she didn't offer herself or thirteen-year-old daughter to help calm the children with him.

"Michael, you must calm yourself to calm the children. We have a situation that could be helped with our connections. I'll check a few things by telephone and get back to you tonight."

Linda called Lance's wife Julie. Linda knew priests needed no reason to be in a hospital at any time. She told Julie the situation before she said, "Have your priest brothers check on Nina's condition and learn the predictions for her recovery. The priests could also suggest a way that could make the hospital want to keep her alive."

Julie said, "That's Michael's daughter. What returns would my family get for this help?"

Linda responded, "Marriage arrangements were made for the children abandoned by your divorced brother. This was done to free your family of troubled lives. Isn't that a lot?"

"My priest brothers could check on the status of Nina's condition. If there's the possibility of survival they could create a desire of the Church to keep her alive. Like other people, the Church does unusual things if it benefits them. My brothers have said that the Church needs more nuns and wants martyrs to help greater beliefs in its religious strengths."

Linda helped to free Stella of the Old Maid label and helped Doctor Robert's dream to become a doctor. Linda kept in touch with Stella's wealthy parents with reminders that her help gave Stella a groom to boast about---and made her parents proud to have a *doctor in their family*. Stella's mother told Linda that Doctor Robert would begin army life in two weeks---right after the Christmas and New Year holidays. She next gave Doctor Robert's home telephone number to Linda who thereafter quickly called him.

Linda told Doctor Robert what Michael told her. As if an order, she told Doctor Robert what she wanted him to do followed with, "Your help as a doctor is needed now! It must be tonight or tomorrow morning at the latest."

"Tomorrow at ten in the morning is when I could be at the hospital but what you asked me to do is against my oath as a doctor."

Linda ignored his objections. "You would tell Jean only what's known about Nina's condition. Jean's free will accepts the likelihood that Nina won't survive, or she accepts what you suggest as the best way to probably save her child from death." Linda ended the telephone without allowing Doctor Robert time to say anything more.

Linda called Michael back: "Nina being in the Catholic hospital is God's way to give us chances for returns from the Church. Our rich families donated much money to the Church, but its priests gave no help with unkept promises of duty marriages into our family group. Instead, the church's priests gave lip service about *free will, help to countrymen and continued donations to the church*. Here's the plan: No one go to the hospital until tomorrow morning when only Jean goes. An eight-year-old child is more attached to the mother than to other family. All is arranged for Jean's arrival at the hospital's Information Desk about ten o'clock tomorrow morning where she'll be surprised at who meets her there." Linda ended the call before Michael could ask who would meet Jean there.

Before Jean and Lewis returned home from his birthday party, Michael told Tricia, "You and I are in a difficult situation to explain how the accident happened. Let's make a father-daughter agreement to protect each other from blame. I won't say the accident happened after you pulled down Nina's starched dress. You won't say I left my children alone for any reason except to use the bathroom on this floor. This way, neither of us are faulted for the accident."

"It sounds good to me. Neither one of us could tell on the other without risks."

Michael nor Tricia thought about who might be blamed for Nina's accident. Neither of them said anything when all family blamed Nina's accident on Lucy's unkept promise to help Michael with the children. Lucy ultimately suffered severe guilts and blames for Nina's accident.

Nina Is Abandoned

Nina was kept on a gurney in the hospital emergency room while staff waited for her parents. Many hours passed without the arrival of her parents. Nina was temporarily put into a private room on the children's floor.

Emma was the long-time governess for children of Michael and Jean who arrived at her usual morning start time on the next day. Her skin color was the product of an African father who was a physician and his wife a Caucasian nurse. As Jean continued to dress, she told Emma, "Nina had an accident last night and is in the hospital. I must be at the hospital at ten o'clock this morning to learn about her condition and medical care needs."

At the Information Desk in the hospital lobby, Jean was more than surprised to be greeted by her childhood friend Robert. They last saw each other when he attended her wedding about thirteen years ago. She believed that his dream to become a doctor came true because he was now in clothes worn by emergency room physicians.

"Please follow me. During the walk to our destination, we can catch up with what has happened in our lives since your wedding day."

When Nina awakened for today, she saw and heard people walk pass her room: nurses, nurse aides, volunteers, men in clothes worn by emergency room staff, men in business suits, and food trays pushed through the hallway. Through all that noise and activity, Nina heard her mother's voice get louder and closer to her room.

A blanket over an arched metal structure covered Nina's stomach area. She could turn on only the unburned side of her body to face the room's doorway as her mother's voice became more distinct. When her mother was at the doorway, the back of her head was against the door's outer frame as she looked up to the tall man who spoke to her as he faced and looked to Nina. He was dressed in clothes worn by emergency room doctors that made Nina believe he was a doctor.

Nina saw this man's face clearly each time he looked directly at her. She saw him look at her raised arm with a waving hand to prove she wasn't in a coma as he told her mother. Nina didn't know why this man ignored her proof of consciousness, why didn't tell her mother she wasn't in a coma, nor why he didn't walk her mother to her [Nina's] bedside.

This doctor often looked at papers in his hand as he talked to Nina's mother. New hallway traffic didn't make it possible for Nina to hear what he was saying to her mother. Hallway traffic again temporarily ended when Nina clearly heard what he said to her mother, but she couldn't hear what her mother said to him:

"She can't survive these serious injuries. Her flesh was burned to the bone on one hip. Her wool sweater kept the flames from quick damage to more of her body. She's had some expected permanent nerve damage. She's in and out of a coma. She wouldn't know who may be at her bedside. You can't do anything for her but you can do what's needed for your other children at home. Life goes on. Life is for the living. It's just a matter of time to when this one is gone. The hospital will contact you to collect the body when it happens. Your signature on this paper gives this hospital permission to do whatever it deems best for this child while still alive."

He continued to speak while Jean signed the paper: "Don't look back to feel more pain about the situation. Walk with me as I put this signed document where it should be and then I'll walk you to the bus stop. I'll stay with you until you are on the bus back to your home." [Nina was the only witness to Doctor Robert's medical wrongdoing.]

The next day, Nina was moved out of the private room into a big room for children where she was quickly surrounded with many young men and one older man who spoke to them at her bedside. A hospital nurse saw Nina's frightened face and rushed to the nun in charge of hospital operations, Sister Rise, who was quickly at Nina's bedside. Sister Rise was dressed in the nun's habit; she was taller than the average woman. The only visible parts of this nun were her hands and a pretty face without face make-up. In a firm voice, Sister Rise asked the medical instructor: "What is this about? Why is this happening?"

The instructor gave Sister Rise the signed document that made Nina a medical guinea pig. After a look at it, Sister Rise told him and his students, "This should have been checked with me before used. It's clear that a mistake was made. It's always been clear that this hospital does not use humans as guinea pigs. I'll find out who and how this happened. Starting now, do nothing with or for this child unless I give detailed written permission."

After the men left, Sister Rise sat at Nina's bedside with many questions: "Please tell me what could help this hospital to help you. How did your injuries happen? Was an adult in charge then? Who cared for you until the ambulance arrived? Do you have poor parents?" Nina answered each question as it was asked. She said her parents were very wealthy. She said she and her siblings were cared for by a governess while her parents worked in their business but only her father was with her and three younger siblings on the accident night.

Sister Rise sympathetically said, "Recalling all you've told must be painful. If you don't feel well enough to continue now, I could come back later today, after you've had a nap."

"I do feel tired. I should feel better after a nap."

"I'll return with nurses and nuns that were stationed on this floor when you were in the private bedroom. I want them to hear your description of your mother and the man with her. One or more of them might be able to recognize the doctor you describe to help us find him."

"Thanks for letting me know your next visit won't be alone. It helps to keep me from being frightened again with many people around me at the same time."

"Instead of after an afternoon nap, we'll be here after your evening meal. God Bless you."

When Sister Rise returned with the hospital staff, Nina described the man with her mother as tall, medium weight, dark blonde color hair, blue eyes, and dressed in clothes like what was worn by emergency room doctors. She described her mother as average height and weight with dark black wavy hair and hazel color eyes.

Nina added, "My mother has an uncle and cousins who are medical doctors, but this man didn't look like any of them."

"What could help this hospital is what you recall and tell me about the signed document that gave you to our research unit."

After Nina described what she heard, Sister Rise and the hospital staff with her almost simultaneously said, "A doctor's first duty is to do no harm and for the comfort and good welfare of a patient. He shouldn't be a doctor with this proof that he failed duties that were important parts of his medical training years." All left the room except one nurse who moved Nina's bed close to windows in the children's ward. From here, Nina could see people going in and out the hospital's front doors. This was to let her see when her parents and other members of her big family would be visiting her now that Christmas was only five days away.

Sister Rise made daily visits to Nina's bedside into New Year day. In one visit, she asked Nina, "Do you know any reason why none of your large family has visited you yet?"

Nina held back tears as she said, "I don't know. I don't know why."

Early the next morning, a group of praying nuns stopped in front of the children's ward where Nina was fixed. They added prayers for visits from Nina's parents and other family. The parents of other children in the room with Nina complained to Sister Rise about the unwanted effects to their children from the early morning prayer stops. The parents reminded this nun that they paid all medical costs for their children without use of charity funds. Thereafter, the prayer stops for Nina were discontinued

Sister Rise mailed a request to Nina's parents for one or both visit her. A request was also mailed to Nina's godparents, Linda and Paul. The mailings listed the long hours that Sister Rise would be in the hospital but didn't give the reason for this request.

Michael telephoned Linda to tell her about the mail from Sister Rise. Linda didn't tell him that she also received the same request from Sister Rise. Nor did Linda tell Michael that she receives reports about Nina's condition from Julie whose priest brothers kept her informed.

Linda told Michael, "Whatever the reason for the nun's note, only Jean makes the trip to the hospital tomorrow. Your time is needed for your business doors to be open for customers."

Michael interrupted. "Wait! I want Jean to hear what you say. I'll put the telephone between us for both of us to hear what you say at the same time."

Linda repeated her words and then said, "The note doesn't fix a time to be there. This allows Jean time to dress slowly and to feel calm before she's with the nun in the hospital. Jean should be well groomed and not in everyday clothes worn for your business. People at the hospital's Information Desk would let the nun know when Jean is there. Hospital staff would take Jean to the nun's office, or the nun would go to where Jean waits. Jean should listen but not respond to what the nun says unless a response is absolutely needed. Jean signs nothing until a lawyer of our choice reviews it and says it's okay to sign."

Jean showed the mail she received to the hospital Information Desk worker who telephoned Sister Rise to inform her that Jean was there. Sister Rise soon greeted Jean in the hospital lobby: "Good Morning. I am Sister Rise, in charge of hospital operations. Please follow me."

Jean didn't know why they used an elevator when the hospital operations office is usually on the first floor. She thought they were headed to where dead bodies were temporarily held. They were soon at the doorway of the large children's ward where a nurse was giving morning medications to patients. Sister Rise spoke to Jean, "Please stop here with me here. Look inside this big room. Your daughter is in the bed nearest to the windows. From there, she could see when her parents and other family might come to visit her.

Nina heard the nun's familiar voice and was able to turn enough to face the doorway."

Jean listened and looked without speaking.

"Why don't you ask to be at your daughter's bedside now? Why do you act as if your child isn't here? No eight-year-old child could be guilty of anything so bad to be punished in this way. She's left to stand alone with every desperate need that doesn't even happen to orphans. No punishment is greater than for parents and other family to totally abandonment a child who grew up with them for eight years. It's a betrayal of love and trust. On top of all else, she has nothing familiar to ease her first time away from all family: no favorite doll, none of her personal bedclothes, and not her own toothbrush.

"Why do you stand with me and respond to nothing? Christmas has come and gone but your daughter has had no visitors, no gifts, no cards or letters from her family. Not even a telephone call to the hospital by any of her family for the status of her condition. It's also not normal that this child hasn't received get well cards or letters from her schoolteacher and classmates as done for other hospitalized children at all times of the year."

Sister Rise's voice became louder as she continued to lose patience with Jean's behavior. "Why hasn't your husband come to the hospital? As her biological father and head of the household, it is his duty to arrange all the needed care for this bedridden child.?"

Except for Sister Rise and Jean, everyone in this area and in this room was so quiet that Nina could hear all said between the nun and her mother. Jean turned around to not face the room full of children when she responded in a stressed and louder than usual voice: "My husband works long hours in our business to provide for us. I have four other children at home who need more of my time since the loss of our governess. She cared for our children and did some of the housework while I shared the work in my husband's business. My brothers and sisters have wage paying work and other reasons why they can't help with my children. My youngest sister is seventeen years old; she lives with and cares for our aging parents and shops with our mother who speaks very little English."

Sister Rise's voice was barely controlled as she continued: "This child needs to know that her family loves and cares about her. She needs their comfort and companionship. Her brothers and sister have each other and family that surround them, while this child is treated like a throw-away. It's important to use this situation to teach your growing children to be compassionate and caring people. Without such training, they'll be selfish and care about only their own lives. Turn around and look at your bedridden child. Realize how much she needs her mother. She can't sit up on her own and is not able to turn much in bed without help. Her food trays are often returned with little if anything consumed. She knows milk is important for good health but has refused it until it was mixed with chocolate."

With a loud stressed voice, Jean said, "She must be punished for having had the accident!"

Sister Rise continued to lose control: "An accident is not something to be punished! This child said you have a maternal uncle and cousins who are doctors. This hospital couldn't check to see if those doctors practiced here because she didn't know their family name. But their choice of the medical arena should have made them know what's been done to this child is perverted! If they visited this child, she would have recognized them as part of her family---but not even they visited this child since she was admitted into this hospital. You wear expensive clothes and jewelry, but the conduct of this child's parents and her big family are some proof that even the rich have all type and class of people."

Jean's response was retaliatory: "People who wear the cloth are no different from people who face life instead of running from it."

Sister Rise quickly responded, "Hospital work is not running away from life! We see and care for people of all ages and all type of medical issues. We tend to the dyeing and to who dies here. The church gets its share of bad apples but does its best to discharge their vows or get the bad apples to leave on their own. The same is true in the medical world for when a doctor fails the duties with his oath to do no harm and put the comfort and good welfare of patient above all else. Who is the doctor that got your signature on this document? He must be punished for his wrongs as a physician."

The nun opened the document she carried as she continued to speak. "How did he get these papers that are always kept in locked places and not used to make humans a guinea pig? We don't expect anyone to risk self with a confession but expect someone's help to keep things good and right. Your continued silence is a refusal to help. Your families didn't suffer like others did with the recent Great Depression. But, if these medical care costs were too heavy with four growing children at home, we could have made payment plans as done for people with less costly medical needs. Mail was sent to this child's rich godparents that asked them to join you for this meeting. Since you came alone, it clearly indicates they refused duties expected of godparents. The whole picture tells me that it's not just a matter of money. Who and what's behind these things? Why do you let yourself be used and punished for such wrongs? What's being done would be unbelievable to who wasn't part of having arranged it or who didn't witness it. It's so rare and unbelievable that it will be a permanent part of our records as proof that it did happen. Your type would probably find ways to remove these records at some time, but there might always be someone who witnessed this and could tell about it."

Jean asked, "Why do we discuss things here instead of in your private office?"

"Talk in these open places doesn't matter. There's been constant gossip about it throughout the hospital. We can't control gossip that travels out of this hospital by staff, patients and their visitors, or whoever visits in this hospital for whatever reason. What your child hears between us wouldn't matter since she has already accepted rejection as part of life."

Without any further response or even a polite goodbye, Jean walked away from Sister Rise. She left the hospital for the bus trip home where she reported all to Michael and Linda.

Jean was out of the hospital when Sister Rise went to Nina's bedside. "What happened here doesn't prove that nuns must be tolerant, patient, forgiving, and obedient to vows and all that services God. I know what happened would be unforgettable for you.

God knows that what's been done and said is unforgivable and needs my prayers for His forgiveness. I behaved in ways that not even I would have expected from any God serving human, but we are humans who try to do God's work. We know He forgives temporary loss of our doing what He wants from us."

Nina again held back tears as she said, "I have no family now. I'm all alone in life now."

"Nuns and priests would be your sisters, brothers and other family parts for as long as you want and need us. We realize you're now left unable to trust anyone in life and even we, who are committed to God's work, must prove trustworthy to you. You are now again God's child as you were before birth. God isn't fickle like some humans. He's always your Holy Father and always there when needed. Church funds will provide for your everyday needs, medical care, and for an education as done for the orphaned children with us. You tell us when and if you decide to enter the convent. Even with vows of poverty, nuns and priests are provided with all that's needed into retirement years and burial costs when God calls."

Sister Rise saw Nina look at the covered metal brace over her body and then at the leg that burn injuries forced to stay bent. Sister Rise answered Nina's unasked question, "With time, patience and our help, you could someday walk again and be active with some normalcy."

The next day, Nina saw Sister Rise with a few nuns and two priests at the nurses' station in front of the children's room with Nina. The priests were gone when Nina heard what was said by Sister Rise and the nuns who all remained with her at this nurses' station:

"Her age and bedridden condition make the mold possible."

"The church could always use a martyr."

"She's too young to understand what that means."

"Survival of these injuries make it believable that she could survive whatever the church assigned for her."

Sister Rise concluded: "Nothing could save the toddler here whose whole body suffered when put into the tub filled with extremely hot water. However, something could be done for this other child. Her wool sweater helped to slow down the flames until her father used his jacket to smother the flames. I've heard that Doctor Bernstein has successfully cared for children with burn injuries across this country. He's been known to care for children whose parents couldn't afford his fees. It's possible that Doctor Bernstein may do the same in this situation. A search will be made to locate him and seek his help for this child."

Doctor Bernstein willing serviced Nina's medical needs without a financial charge. He needed to perform more than one skin graft surgery. Skin grafts were taken from both of Nina's thighs above knee level, with time for the skin to heal between surgeries. The healing process caused strong urges to scratch. To prevent scratching, gloves were tied to Nina's hands before tied to the bed's back posts during the healing process. No hospital staff could be given duty to comfort Nina during these times but nurses in different work shifts checked on her. Nina was temporarily put into a private room near to the nurses' station during each recovery period.

Gossip about Nina's abandonment was quickly passed from children not yet discharged and their visitors to incoming patents and their visitors. Nina couldn't stop

visitors who used her abandonment as an example of what could happen to their children

who might misbehave. Nina stopped explaining how her accident happened when the

children and their visitors refused to believe her truths about the night of her accident.

Nina's privacy was hurt when some children in the ward with her and their

visitors lifted the covers atop her arched metal frame to look at her injured body. It

happened was less often when she kept her eyes open during daytime naps. Nina couldn't

stop the children from throwing paper planes at her when no adults could see---planes

made from the pages of their coloring books. Nina also could not stop the children that

repeatedly said, "No one cares about her. We can do anything to her that's fun for us".

These painful experiences caused Nina to cry. Children in the room increased

their harassment with the label "cry baby" and made fun at her belief in Santa Claus. The

variant of abuses became everyday life for Nina who looked for its end when she was no

longer bedridden. Although for short periods of time, she had some acceptable

conversation with the medical and hospital staff who cared for her.

With aims to calm Nina, nuns and priests spoke to her about the sufferings of Jesus

as he died on the cross. They told her about the names and labels given to their religious

clothes when in public places: "Some children and adults refer to nuns as *penguins*. Some

children and adults make fun of the long skirts priests wear at the altar."

Different clergy preached to Nina that abandonment returned her to God. With her

plans to become a nun, they spoke to her about the qualities God needed. Nuns and

priests took turns to tell Nina, "God works in mysterious ways. He gives us many

chances to prove worthy of the earthly duties He assigns."

Reclaiming Nina

New Year Day has passed; children are back in school. Neighbors began to question Michael and Jean about why Nina wasn't seen during the holidays---and why she wasn't seen going to school. Michael, Jean and their children at home pretended to not have heard the questions about Nina. Some neighbors assumed that Nina had an illness that caused her death and it was still painful for her family to talk about it. This assumption was dismissed when there was no sign of a funeral as was the ways of their church and of their ethnic group of people.

Michael and Jean found it increasingly difficult to provide for their family as the number of customers dwindled. They didn't think that anything or anyone hurt their business. The only help Linda gave them was instructions about what to tell their four children at home about their sister [Nina]: "Tell your children Nina survived but it is uncertain for how much longer she'd continue to live. Let children at home continue life normally. When school children ask them about Nina, they should change the conversation's subject. Jean should tell neighbors and school staff what she was first told---that Nina's injuries are so severe she's not expected to survive, and if she died, the hospital would let you know when to reclaim her body. It omits much but none of it is a lie." Such talk made school staff and school children believed that Nina was dying.

On a Sunday that neither Michael or Jean attended church services, neighbors told them, "Today's priest added prayers for Nina's continued survival and a miracle for her total recovery. He said only the name Nina, but we know one of your daughters is named Nina and you said she is temporarily away from home." Michael remembered that these neighbors saw the ambulance take Nina out of their home on the accident night. What neighbors now told him helped him to consider a possibility that his business was blacklisted to punish the abandonment. His mixed emotions were guilt with anger when he telephoned Linda and told her:

"As baptismal godmother for two of my children, you need to know that I need help to provide for my family! Jean and I followed your advice to tell neighbors and school staff that Nina's survival is uncertain. And your advice to tell neighbors the heavy costs for her medical care hurt our lives. People refused to believe we paid her medical costs when I we had no proof with receipts from the hospital that show dates and amounts paid. People have said that a proper first decision would have increased the number of customers to us, and that people would have helped in different ways. Linda, what was done was carried out with your insistence for all to stick together as a united family. It was your belief the church owed for huge donations from our families when it refused to help with the unkept duty marriages. Following what you asked has made only my family unit become poverty-stricken and in need of help."

"Michael, what's done is done, but I didn't force you to follow what I believed." Michael and Jean received no help of any kind from their separate families. Michael and Jean continued to accept Linda as their matriarch and to follow her telephone instructions:

"Michael, taxes we must pay is part of public funds used to help people in need. Your family with growing children is now in need of that help. A doctor from your wife's family could help you to qualify for it. The doctor's letter would say you suffer heart issues without giving it a diagnostic name---that your condition required much rest with reduced stress before your return to work. A letter worded this way would not make the doctor guilty of any wrong."

Jean's maternal uncle Doctor Andrew wrote the letter.

Michael and Jean received the first monthly public funds in the month of May. They were then told that all recipients would be re-evaluated in January to determine if they qualified for continued funds in addition to wearing apparel and footwear for growing children. Thanksgiving Day repeated the usual holiday meal in the home of Linda and Paul but now with only the family of Michael and Jean. After the meal, Michael told Linda: "January is not far away. That's when a re-evaluation will decide if public funds to us will end or continue. This process would require another letter from the doctor. We doubt he could extend the time for me to recover from a heart issue without proof I was hospitalized for it. We don't know how we could provide for our family without this income since our business profits remain minimal."

"The first thing is to rebuild bonds with Nina in the hospital. Jean is to visit Nina while your other children are in school. Jean no longer dresses like a woman of wealth when she goes to the hospital now. She and your toddler son Jerry go there with the doll I will buy for Nina. If staff in the lobby refuse to permit Jerry as a visitor, Jean asks to speak with Sister Rise. The nun and Jean talk about her visit to Nina with Jerry. We need to know how that goes before we could move further."

The hospital information staff informed Sister Rise that Jean was there with a toddler child. The nun met Jean in the lobby. "Welcome. Please follow me to my office where we could privately talk about why you are here." On the way to the office, Sister Rise asked, "Who is this handsome boy with you? Who is to have the doll in your arm that is almost as big as this child?"

"This is my youngest of five children, Jerry. He is two years old and recently began to walk. He was too heavy before then to stay on his feet for too long. Life is much easier now that he doesn't have to be carried most of the time that he's awake. This doll is a belated birthday gift for my daughter Nina who turned nine years old this past August. Her love of dolls stayed in the minds of all family. This doll is to let her know she was never forgotten."

When inside the office, Sister Rise found a chair for Jerry to sit on instead of only on his mother's lap. She found a small toy car to keep him busy while she and Jean talked. As Sister Rise reached the chair behind her desk, she told Jean, "Please be seated and tell me the purpose of this unexpected visit."

Jean used ways of The Family to not waste words. "My daughter Nina has been in this hospital for eleven months. I'm here to reclaim her. My husband and I want her back in our home before Christmas."

"But why now after near to a year since she was abandoned?"

"Nina was never abandoned in the strict meaning of the word. The ambulance took her from our home to here. The hospital is a place of shelter with qualified people for her care and needs. Situations at home needed attention before we could have her back with us."

"The separate families of your husband and you are more than enough for some among them to have helped with your children at home so you could have spent time here with Nina. If none were able to help for whatever reason, it doesn't explain why none of this child's big family have visited her in all these months. No visits, no cards, no letters, no gifts, and no telephone calls to this hospital to ask about her condition. *This is known as total abandonment.*"

Jean calmly said, "Few families are without trouble in some way, at some time in life. Our families work out our own troubles. We are now able for Nina to be back home with her family."

"Nothing helps to understand why Nina experienced total abandonment. Things don't fit right. This matter must be decided in Family Relations Court. While we wait for ——— when this would be on the court calendar, it would be good for you and Nina to reconnect as mother and daughter. You may take this child with you only today. After this exception to hospital rules, your visits must be during normal visiting hours and with only healthy children of fourteen years and older."

Jean and her toddler son took the elevator to the second-floor children's ward. As they entered the room, Jean saw Nina's confused look before she turned her head away from her brother and mother

Jean was at Nina's bedside when she spoke: "I was given special permission to bring your brother Jerry to visit you. He finally learned to walk; it made life easier. Look at how well he walks in front of these windows. His ability to walk has helped him to lose the weight that had slowed down his past ability to walk."

Nina's trembling voice said, "He was a little over one year old when he last saw me. How could he now know who I am or that he had another sister? Why should I reconnect with him to again risk broken bonds like my family has done to me? Why are you here now?"

Jean sat on the chair at Nina's bedside. "I'm here to begin things for your return home."

"I don't want to go back to a family that proved to care nothing about me in any way."

"Attention was needed for a lot of different family issues that happened since your accident. Most of it has been taken care of with a few big changes in our lives. Knowing you were in good hands made it possible to take care of the big things before your return home."

"Why did you let that doctor talk you into what's been done to me? Why did you let him keep your back to me? Why didn't you come to my bedside before you walked away with him? I heard what he said to you about my condition then. If that did prove true, why didn't you come to me for a last *goodbye between us*?"

"Your many questions are not easy to answer. I'll try to do it in my next visit to you."

"Why not answer now? Do you need time to think about what to explain or not explain---to think about what I would or wouldn't believe?"

"Answers to your questions should be without interruptions. As you can see, Jerry goes from a look out these windows back onto my lap. Picking up what's said before interruptions wouldn't make it easy to explain things."

"I see no reason for you to come back. Nothing could change what I've been through alone except for visits from nuns and priests. My family's behavior spoke louder than words."

"I'll visit you alone tomorrow to talk things out." Jean rose from the chair and held Jerry's hand as they went to the elevator and to their bus trip home. Jean and Jerry were out of the building when Sister Rise went to Nina. She wanted Nina's fresh reactions to time spent with her mother and youngest brother. Without a comment now, Sister Rise listened to all Nina said.

Family Court Ruled in Favor of Parents

Jean told Michael about her visit with Sister Rise and with Nina. They telephoned Linda before their children were home from school. Michael shared the telephone with Jean for them to hear what Linda had to say at the same time: "Don't prepare the children at home for Nina's return until the matter is decided by a court of law. Jean should make daily visits alone to Nina. Jean's visits to the hospital would make everyone see Nina's mother. Daily visits quiet claims that no one cares about Nina. It quiets use of her abandonment as an example of punishment for other children. Jean, you keep busy with crotchet work at Nina's bedside for when she won't interact with you. You explain to nurses assigned to the children's room why you can't visit every day and why you can't stay the full length of visiting hours. Along the way, you show the nurses your appreciation of their care of Nina with gifts of the handkerchiefs with your crotched edgings. Other times you do it with cash gifts that we'd give you for the nurses. But another gift for Nina must wait for until we know her use of time while bedridden."

During Jean's next visit to the hospital, Nina showed no changed feelings for her mother or her big family. Most of the time, Jean sat quietly in a chair at Nina's bedside with crochet work in hand. Jean used some time to talk with nurses assigned to the room with Nina in it.

Nina suddenly looked at her mother and asked, "Why are you here again?"

"I want us to rebuild our mother and daughter relationship. I want to keep my promise to answer your questions."

"I remember that I asked you to explain things. I also remember that I said nothing could erase the actions of my big family when I was in desperate need of them in every way. I've learned to live without the family I grew up with. I've learned to accept life alone in this world. I don't want to go back to a family that proved to be of no good value when needed."

"You've been here with nuns for eleven months. This experience must have taught you that forgiveness is a needed part of life. If family's errors are unforgivable, see your experiences here as what strengthens you for ongoing life---and give good credit to your family for this. When grown, you'll learn that life isn't a steady handful of roses for anyone."

"Who and what strengthened me are the nuns and priests who gave me strong belief and trust in God. I heard you tell Sister Rise that I must be punished for having had the accident. *The* word *accident* made it clear that it didn't require the punishment given to me. I don't want to constantly fear punishment if I had another accident. I heard Sister Rise tell you, *as you sow so shall you reap.* You know it means that my multiple traumatic experiences alone mean I owe nothing to any of my family when they need or want it. I owe nothing to the family I was born into or to extended family of my family."

"Nina, your schoolteachers help students know when they've made mistakes and help students know how to correct their mistakes. Grownups also make mistakes and correct those mistakes as best as possible to go on with life."

"A teacher's help to correct mistakes is good for the student. A growing child's life is forever hurt when a whole family makes mistakes as big as what's been done to me. I'm only nine years old but don't feel like a child. I don't even know what a child of my age is like."

"Nina, tell me what and how life has been for you here. Start with when the ambulance took you to this hospital into now."

Jean sat quietly with crochet work at Nina's bedside to hear all Nina told. Nina ended with a repetition of her earlier words: "Only nuns and priests cared about me in all the time I've been alone and bedridden. Someday, I'm going to be a nun. I still want to know about the man with you at the doorway of my bedroom the day after I was taken here. I want to know why you didn't come to my bedside to look at me before you left with that man."

"That man was one of my school classmates before I married your father. My family and his family were neighbors and friends who were guests at my wedding. He and I lost tract of each other until we met here. On the way to the bedroom you were in, we told each other how our lives progressed after my wedding day. I learned that his dream to be a doctor happened and I felt proud that he remembered me."

Jean sensed it was best to leave before she said more than already said about him. The large room for children with their visitors was not soundproof. Talks between Jean and Nina could have been heard by everyone in this room and what was said could reach Sister Rise.

Jean was well out of the hospital when Sister Rise re-visited Nina to learn about today's time with her mother. After Nina told about the doctor who was with her mother, Sister Rise said, "This hospital needs to know more! One of the nurses on duty here tomorrow will let me know when your mother is with you so I can discuss things with her."

The next day, a nurse notified Sister Rise when Jean was at Nina's bedside. With papers in hand, Sister Rise quickly went to Nina's bedside and sat on the chair next to Jean. The nun's voice was soft but tense as she spoke to Jean: "It's good that you could make the visits to Nina." Sister Rise showed Jean the document for guinea pig uses and then said, "I've already explained to you how Nina knows about her situation. It makes it acceptable to discuss an issue with you here. The hospital needs your help in connection with this document. Is this your signature?"

Jean looked at the paper and with a weak voice said, "Yes, that's my signature. I didn't examine what I signed. I trusted the doctor who said my daughter couldn't survive the injuries. I believed him when he said she was in and out of a coma and unable to know who was at her bedside or in the room with her."

"But you personally know this doctor who had you sign this instrument? These papers are kept in locked places and never used to make guinea pigs of humans. We need to also know who provided this doctor with this instrument to prevent it from being repeated. You were originally from a family that produced doctors. You must have known this doctor's conduct was against all his training years. You must also know that he must be made accountable for such wrongdoing not only for this child but for his continued care of patients. Please write his full name and place of practice on this paper.

This hospital has a duty to report him to the state Medical Board."

Jean realized she said too much and returned to family ways of silence and withholding information and to not put things in writing to possibly increase troubled life. She didn't give the doctor's name or where he practiced. Sister Rise realized Jean would not help in needed ways and walked away.

Michael and Jean received written notice that issues about reclaiming Nina would be heard in Family Court at 9 o'clock on the morning of November twentieth with a copy of the notice to Sister Rise at the hospital. Michael immediately telephoned Linda with the news about the Family Court hearing. Linda said, "I'll call you back after I check out a few things."

Linda again chose Lance's wife Julie for help. Julie could get advice from lawyer Benji who helped his sister and Julie's divorced brother to run off together and avoid compliance with the court ordered for alimony and child support. Lawyer Benji gave Julie the legal loopholes for how Nina could be reclaimed without legal charges against her parents. Julie returned Linda's call with this information. Linda telephoned Michael to give him and Jean the information:

"Good news! You could have a new reason for continued receipt of public funds with Nina back in your home before the January re-evaluation. When in court, you or Jean tell the judge that Nina was left in a sheltered place that was equipped with all needed for her care with no intention to totally abandon her. It is a legal technicality that the judge will accept. This is legal advice from the lawyer who shares troubled life with Julie's family. Use this advice without the cost of a lawyer for a decision that would be in your favor.

"Tell the judge you want Nina home before Christmas to not miss another holiday away from family. Don't say you now collect public funds or that it will soon be re-evaluated. You don't want anything on record for why you now want to reclaim her. Tell the court that Nina must be taught to walk again before discharged from the hospital because you have four other growing children. You don't have to give an accounting of your finances, but you should tell the judge that your financial situation needs continued charity funds for Nina's ongoing care in the hospital's outpatient clinic. Also, ask the court for an end of talks from the nuns to Nina that shame her family and would worsen family life when she's back home. The sitting judge would undoubtedly agree with all things, and court orders must be carried out no matter what."

The judge ruled in favor of Michael and Jean for all issues. The written decision of Family Court was sent to Nina's parents and to Sister Rise at the hospital before Jean's next visit to Nina. Jean was at Nina's bedside when Sister Rise sat on the chair near to her and faced Jean as she spoke. "This hospital could do nothing to change laws that favored Nina's return to parents. A memo to our hospital staff has informed them of the court ruling to end talks to Nina that could worsen her refusal to be reclaimed. This hospital will comply with the court rulings to make Nina able to walk in advance of her discharge before the Christmas holiday. When Nina is discharged, a schedule would be ready and given to you for her continued care in our Out-Patient Clinic. This hospital would also adhere to the court ruling that charity funds would also be used for Nina's continued care in our Out-Patient Clinic." Sister Rise left after a polite *goodbye* to Jean and *God Bless You* to Nina.

Jean was out of the hospital when Sister Rise returned to Nina's bedside. "I'm sorry about the court decision that favored your parents. This hospital and the church could do nothing more than what was done on your behalf. We must forgive who made the wrong decision. The court didn't witness the unbelievable things connected with your situation. The judge couldn't know that the decision was not in your best interests."

"Why didn't I have a say before that decision?"

"In matters such as this, children your age aren't permitted a say about their lives. Time may change these laws. When it does, it could give you the right for a say about your life when you are older. Meanwhile, you must do your best to live peacefully with your family until old enough for your own choices and decisions. God works in mysterious ways. He must have kept you alive for a reason. What's now happening could be one of His tests to determine your strengths to later serve Him. Our help for you to walk again needs to first straighten the leg with burn injury on the thigh's upper part. Next is for you to be on both feet without help from anyone or anything. Food carts are here now. Eat as much as possible and drink the chocolate milk to be strong for all that will start tomorrow morning."

Jean made a few more visits to Nina and continued to be friendly with floor nurses. She again told them about her other children at home and asked for extra care to Nina when she couldn't visit. Jean continued to thank the nurses with gifts of her crocheted handkerchiefs and sometimes cash gifts as Linda instructed. At Nina's bedside, Sister Rise informed Jean about the procedures in use for Nina to walk before discharged.

Jean politely responded, "Thank you for what is being done and will be done for Nina. Let me remind you there is to be no more talk to her against her family or about convent life."

Sister Rise politely told Jean, "I feel a duty to explain some things about Nina before she is back with her family. She'll be like a Babe-In-The-Woods and unable to again survive outside of church life. Her survival of serious injuries is a continuing miracle. It's predictable that her sister and brothers won't accept her return or would not make her feel welcomed back.

"She'll never be able to again fit into her family's way of life, not even if she recalled their ways. She'll always be a misfit among her families and with other people. She'll never again find good value in the family she was born into. She'll never be able to fight her own battles. She'll be taken advantage of and laughed for her different ways. Such reaction and behavior could be from her own family. God knows that we who serve Him are not perfect but her experiences since the accident make her think *she* must be perfect. Nothing and no one could make up for what she has suffered. Nothing could undo the effects to her with abandonment and multiple back-to-back traumatic experiences."

Jean interrupted with a confident voice: "Children adjust and bounce back fast."

Sister Rise replied with a continued soft voice: "Not from this! Her psyche has changed so much that she could never again fit into the outside world as other people do."

Jean repeated, "Children adjust and bounce back fast."

Sister Rise took a deep breath. Her next words were a mixture of self-restraint and inability to hold back what she felt: "This child's family could break the patience of Holy

Saints. This family does things when and if it fits their schedules, not when and as

needed. It's not right to use people or toy with lives, no matter what age or status. You

show up after the hard work is done. Your family's ways with marriages would not give

this child anyone different from selves ---no one to truly care about and be devoted to

her. Your kind destroys anyone and everyone who crosses your paths. She's been

devastated by these experiences and has matured beyond her age. She'll never have the

emotional or physical strength needed for everyday life as others do."

"Are you saying my daughter is retarded or unable to grow into womanhood?"

"No! No! Her experiences here made her ignorant of the life she was born into, but

not retarded or stupid. She has shown intelligence far above the average child of her age.

Another important issue is that your family's ways require marriage to produce children.

Her scarred body could not stretch for full-term pregnancy---and pregnancy would

jeopardize her life. We see no good intentions with reclaiming her. She owes nothing to a

family who sacrificed nothing in her times of every desperate need. She has had only

God's watchful eyes with the care and watchful eyes of we who serve Him."

Jean's voice was confidently strong when she again interrupted: "The church can't

accuse anyone of wrongdoing and is bound to the rules of forgiveness. The church has

been and still is guilty of *cradle snatching* for nuns and priests. To make a martyr of this

child would increase what she has suffered and not prove good intentions. Why wasn't

she kept in a private room to prevent what she suffered from children in this room and

their visitors?"

"This hospital functions as a business. We must account for all money to us,

including use of charity funds. Private rooms bring greater income. Your husband and you operate a business and should have understood this without the need for it to be explained." Sister Rise felt it best to depart but not before she told Jean, "God's wrath will be upon this child's family for taking back what was given to Him. His wrath would spread to whoever deliberately worsens this child's life or allows others to do so at any time. Her experiences have strengthened her for the possibility to outlive her family for her to witness God's mysterious work." Sister Rise left after she politely said *enjoy your day* to Jean and *God is with you* to Nina.

After Jean left the hospital, Sister Rise returned to Nina's bedside. "Most state laws follow the Ten Commandments, but none covered rare things such as these matters. It's predictable that your family would not change. For this reason, and before you leave here, nuns and nurses will instruct you on how to care for yourself without counting on any of your family for help. If you ever feel abused or neglected by your family, seek help in a church nearest to you."

When Jean returned home, Michael telephoned Linda for her to hear Jean's report about today's time in hospital at the same he would also hear it.

Nina's Return to Parental Home

Linda instructed Michael and Jean about how things should be in their home before and after Nina's return to her family. "Make a private room for her. Keep her brothers and sister away from her. Their rough play could accidentally hurt Nina's recovery."

Two weeks before Christmas, the taxi took Nina and her mother from the hospital to where she remembered life with her family. Jean took Nina to the back of the building where they entered the big kitchen behind the retail area of their business. Michael was feeding twenty-eight-month-old Jerry at the kitchen table when he spoke to Nina.

"Your mother is headed upstairs to our apartment home. Sit here next to Jerry an me where there is a glass of chocolate milk and cookies for you. You and I can talk after I clean Jerry's face and hands and give him cleaned pots to play with on the floor near to us."

Michael poured a cup of coffee for himself that he sipped at as he spoke to Nina. "Your mother and I felt it was best for you to be home before your brothers and sister returned from school. You need to know what things happened for our family while you were in the hospital. One of our changes was a move from the third floor down to the second-floor apartment that has an attached front porch. The porch was enclosed and made into a private bedroom for you. This lets you rest or sleep as needed without interruption. Your bedroom has a lot of windows to look out of, as it was for you in the hospital. Your room has a bed, a chair for when you want to sit up, a night table for your personal items with a lamp on top of it, and a small dresser of drawers for bedclothes, underwear and clothes for your trips to and from the hospital clinic. There's a light fixture in the center of the porch bedroom ceiling with a switch on the doorway for you to turn the light on and off. Let your mother and me know if you want or need anything that's not in your room. And if you want anything else that isn't part of your bedroom.

"Your ability to walk again gives you freedom to use the bathroom; it's in the same place as it was in our third-floor home---close to the kitchen back door. With you only one flight above the business and its kitchen, we would always know when you leave the bedroom and where you are above us."

Nina quietly consumed the cookies and milk while her father continued to talk:

"Another change in our lives is that Emmis is no longer our governess and housekeeper. Your mother now prepares all family meals; she and I would deliver each meal to you and clean up after you finish each meal. Let us know what you want us to put in your room for snacks between meals. Every day your room would have a large pitcher of fresh drinking water with a clean glass to drink from. Every day, you will also be given soap, a bowl of clean water, clean washcloths and towels to dry yourself.

"Except for your bathroom needs, there is no need for you to move about much during your recovery. Jerry needs more time before old enough to start school. He will be kept with your mother and me down here to make sure he doesn't accidentally do anything to hurt your healing process. He will be with me when you and your mother take a taxi to and from the hospital's Clinic."

Michael refilled Nina's glass with chocolate milk and refilled his cup with coffee. He took a deep breath to remain calm before he told Nina other family life changes. "There's one more change for our family. Situations forced your parents to apply for public assistance and we receive funds for everyday living costs. Clothes and footwear are provided for our children and includes new sizes with growths. The agency that provides for us fixed a time for me to recover from a heart condition with medical care. We have used this allowed time to rebuild our business to its success of the past years. Your mother, your brothers, sister and I miss the good life and advantages as wealthy people and hope to make it part of our lives again."

Jean returned to the first-floor kitchen. Michael told Nina, "Go upstairs with your mother to your new private bedroom. After you are there, she'll return here to await return of your brothers and sister from school to let them know you are again part of our lives. During your absence, Tricia became the only sister for three brothers, and enjoyed being part of the rough play that's typical of growing boys. Your mother and I will instruct them to keep a distance from you with our concern that their rough play might accidentally hurt your recovery."

Nina was in her bedroom when she heard the excited voices of her brothers and sister. They talked about Christmas gift exchanges as part of classroom parties in school next week, and about school break for Christmas through New Year's Day. She heard nothing for a long time after that when she again heard voices from downstairs. Nina recognized the voice of her sister, Tricia who was two months from her eighth birthday: "Why was she brought back to us? Even at my young age, it's clear that *taking her back hurts everything and everyone---it hurts all of life."*

Michael's voice was quickly heard: "Tricia, keep your voice down. Loud voices carry upward. The doors here and at our second-floor home are open for us to quickly go from one place to another. Think twice before you speak. Be considerate of your sister's feelings."

Tricia didn't lower the volume of her angry words. "I don't care if she does hear me. I never knew what it was like to be without a sister until after her accident. I like being the only sister for my brothers. I don't want to share the bedroom with her again. I like it that no one enters my bedroom without a knock on the door and must wait for my permission to enter."

Michael said, "You're becoming selfish like your Aunt Lucy. Think of the expression *there but for you go I.* Someday you'd need and want your older sister. Don't make it impossible for both of you to again be close sisters who care about each other."

"Her problems aren't mine. Only my life matters to me. I'll never need or want a sister when I'm grown. My life would be filled with a husband, children, and friends we make."

After this, Nina heard nothing more from anyone downstairs.

After only two days home, Nina felt isolated and further rejected by family. When Michael took a meal to her, she asked him, "Why doesn't anyone spend time with me? When in the hospital, I had some form of company with hospital medical staff plus stops of the janitorial staff. Now, my parents have no time except for what's necessary. My brothers and sister don't stop by my room to at least wave hello as the least form of connection. None of our big family visit me. Why am I left alone so much?"

Michael sat on the chair near to where Nina sat up in bed and responded as Linda had instructed: "Your mother and I spend a lot of time to rebuild the business. We must be concerned about the whereabout and activities of your brothers and sister. These things leave little time for your parents to be alone together. You have time with your mother for the trips to and from the Clinic. Your private bedroom is far from bedrooms for the rest of us; it doesn't help your sister and brothers to remember that you are back home. They are busy with friends and activities for their different ages. What keeps them busy frees your parents of worry that their rough-housing ways might accidentally hurt your continued recovery. You have the Bible and Rosary Beads to keep you busy; also, these windows to look out of to see people, cars, buses and trolley cars."

"When at the clinic, my mother rushes to leave immediately after my medical care ends. She allows no time for me to be with any of the nuns I know or the clinic nuns I've gotten to know. My extra time in the clinic would make me feel connected with people. It helps especially since I have no company when home. Being with my mother to and from the clinic isn't the same as having company. She and I barely speak to each other during those taxi trips."

"You have things that keep you busy while alone at home. Think about all your mother must do in one day before and after the trips with you: She makes breakfast, lunch, snacks, and supper for all of us. She helps with the work to rebuild our business. She cleans and tidies our apartment home, the retail shop and kitchen behind it. She checks to see that your brothers and sister haven't wandered far from home."

"Why don't any of my cousins visit? Two of the three sisters are old enough to make the three-block trip together to and from here. They were never into rough house play. With schools closed for the Christmas to New Year's Day holiday, all family's children have some free time."

"The oldest girl of those three cousins, Leslie is sixteen. Her sister, Paula is thirteen and Nancy is ten years old. Their parents give them duties in their tavern business to always know where they are. The girls serve lunch and supper to customers, clean the tables that customer leave, plus clean up duties in the tavern's kitchen. Their tavern is closed on Sundays but is another busy day for them. They go to church as a family. After church, the three girls work at their grooming needs such as cutting or trimming fingernails and toenails and putting nail polish on those nails. Nancy is too young to travel alone to and from here. Leslie and Paula spend time making the clothes they wear. When school reopens after the holidays, these sisters will need Sundays for their extra school homework. This is truer for Leslie and Paula who want to keep the high marks they always had."

"What about my godmother's daughter Lynn? Parents never allowed her to help in their restaurant business. She's old enough for a trip alone to and from here with a short bus ride."

"Lynn is only thirteen years old. Parents keep her busy with duties to clean and tidy their large apartment above their business. Lynn must also iron the cleaned shirts that her brothers and father wear every day. Her parents won't let her travel alone with public transportation because they know the ways of many public transportation drivers who eat in their diner. Lynn's parents also heard about some bad things that happen on public transportation. Lynn's parents feel it's too long a walk for her to make alone to and from here even in daylight hours."

"What about my aunts and uncles, my mother's sisters and brothers? They are grown adults who have not yet married. Aunt Lucy, Uncle Rocco and Uncle Caesar live with their parents around the block from us."

"Your Uncle Rocco and Uncle Caesar have wage paying work with long hours. They need weekends to relax in recreational ways as young men do. Your Aunt Lucy stays home with their aging parents, your grandparents. She helps with the English language when their mother shops. Your mother's other sister, your Aunt Sarah lives in a nearby state and is very busy as breadwinner and caregiver of her three growing sons. If your Aunt Sarah could make a trip to and from here, her travel time would be longer than the time she could have here."

"There is always some reason why I must be left alone. I need more to occupy time than just the Bible, Rosary Beads, and windows to look out of. Maybe books from the public library for me to read plus a dictionary for words in books I don't know yet."

"For now, we'll let you be the first to read comic books bought for your brother Lewis. As the oldest of our children, he normally reads them before they are passed to younger ones. Later we'd have books for you from the library where a librarian knows what books are read by girls your age."

When Lewis learned that the comic books were given to Nina first, she heard his very loud complaint to their parents: "Why did you make her the first to read my comic books? I'm the first-born who is always first in line for that and everything else."

Michael said, "You must learn there are times when you can't and won't be first with or for everything. It's an important lesson for when you are an adult in the outside working world. Calm down. Your Aunt Lucy would soon have books from the library for Nina."

"I'll think about losing first place in a workplace when the time comes. Right now, I don't want to lose my place as the oldest of your children and first in line for everything. Aunt Lucy should be fast with books for Nina. I don't want my place as first in line to be forgotten."

* * * * * * * * * * * *

On a Sunday afternoon, Michael was downstairs alone with work for his business. Four of his children played games in the open area behind the kitchen. Nina was not fully asleep for her long afternoon nap when she was awakened by the unusually loud voice of her mother in the far-off kitchen of their second-floor kitchen: "Lucy, you're following in ——— the same paths as Sarah for the same troubles that hurt her life and shamed our family." Lucy's active social life helped her forget her severe guilt and blames for Nina's accident a little more than a year ago.

Sarah was sixteen years old when she was arranged to have a child out of wedlock as punishment for having refused duty to be the bride of Michael's younger brother Lance. Sarah was blamed for her one-year old son's death with pneumonia. She later had two more sons with a common law husband that increased the shame for her siblings and parents who did not approve of this lifestyle. Twenty-two-year-old Sarah now faced Jean:

"I'm not a nun and never had plans to enter a convent! I didn't plan to drop out of school to support a child! I don't like being family's black sheep or outcast! Our lives were cursed with your wedding that mixed us with the wrong type and kind of people! It doesn't matter who said what for you to marry when fourteen years old. No weapon was used to force you to marry an opposite of all ways and things from our birth families. You're lucky that all your children have the good looks and nice shapes of our family and nothing like their father and his families---especially not like the girl who looks and acts like a monkey. Lucy and I have wondered how you'd feel if our cursed lives fell upon you and your children! The Bible does say things pass from one generation to the next."

Eighteen-year-old Lucy interrupted with a voice as fierce as Sarah's. "Your wedding opened the door for your husband's family to financially provide better lives for your younger siblings and parents that became a debt. Although the debt of our parents, your brothers and sisters were arranged with duty marriages to pay the debt when old enough to marry. It should not have been the duty of growing children to pay the debt of parents this way. Grown children should not be expected to give up all of life for the debts of parents!"

"Sarah. Lucy. I'm your older sister who took care of you for many years before I married. I had no reason to deliberately hurt your lives with my wedding. Nothing before my wedding let me know it would trouble your lives. You've both already blamed other family and the church for your hurt lives. Maybe you both needed to again vent your feelings and I was chosen for it."

Lucy said, "Ignorance was no excuse. Family of our parents say they have nothing to do with the matters connected to our parents and us. Jean, there is a way to make amends for how your wedding hurt our lives. You would do it without your husband's permission. One of yours [daughters] could take my duty to be the bride of Linda's son.

Our brothers have no objection to this replacement of me. If you agree, I'd make it start to happen when both girls are in school.

"When the time is right, our brother Rocco would work for Lance to have a bride to also calm his anger about no returns for spent money." Sarah and Lucy had nothing more to discuss and left Jean without attempts to visit Nina.

* * * * * * * * * * * * *

Nina's multiple traumatic experiences and long absence from family life made her forget their ways with life. She couldn't understand what she overheard between her mother and aunts. Since returned to parents, what she read in the Bible and books from the library made her see life in very different ways than how her family lived. The lives of nuns and what Nina read added to what she witnessed with family of hospitalized children in the big room with her.

Books from the library given to Nina were about women who did more with life than to be a wife and mother: Madame Curie was a chemist who pioneered the research on radioactivity. Florence Nightingale didn't marry and didn't wear the religious cloth, but her life was much like that of a nun. Women authored books that were in schools and in public libraries. Books helped Nina to know there are good and honest ways to fill life without marriage and whether she did or didn't become a nun.

Nina was near to her eleventh birthday when discharged from continued medical care. Family allowed her to make the Church Confirmation sacrament. Linda assigned her nearly fifteen-year-old daughter Lynn to be Nina's sponsor. Linda was Nina's baptismal godmother and Lynn now to become Nina's Confirmation sponsor-godmother.

Linda celebrated the occasion with a family gathering in the large open area behind her family diner business. Guests were Nina's siblings and parents, birth families of her parents and their extended parts. Guests included Wayne, Bertha and their three daughters. As usual, Aunt Lucy was keenly attentive to all said and done.

Millie and her three children were not invited even though the arranged marriages were to make them part of these families. Lance and Julie didn't attend with their toddler son; they still felt the pain of Michael's boasts about his beautiful wife and children on their wedding day.

———

Blood Connected and Not Connected

Mothers of Linda and Bertha were sisters and made them blood tied first cousins of each other. Children of Linda and Paul and children of Wayne and Bertha were blood connected second cousins.

There were no blood ties to connect children of Linda and Paul with children of Lance and Julie.

There were no blood ties to connect children of Michael and Jean with children of _______ Linda and Paul.

Blood ties connected children of Michael and Jean with children of Wayne and Bertha and with children of Lance and Julie.

Children of divorced Millie and children produced by Lance and Julie were first-cousin blood ties of each other.

Nina's Return to School

Labor Day weekend has passed, and the Fall school term is now in the first week of classes. With nearly three years out of school, Nina's return required tests for her grade level. Test results showed an intelligence score of a twenty-one-year-old instead of her eleven years. School staff offered Nina's parents two choices for her continued education: (1) Let her skip grades for studies to challenge her in classes with children older than she is, or (2) Put her in the fifth grade with children her age but studies less challenging and discomfort with children who wouldn't like a student smarter than they are.

All family were curious about Nina's return to school: Wayne, Bertha, their three daughters, Linda, Paul and their three offspring, Nina's four siblings, and Aunt Lucy. Michael and Jean answered everyone's questions. Linda again used her matriarch role to advise Michael and Jean about a grade level choice for Nina:

"It's clearly best for her to be in the fifth grade. It would help her to socialize with children her age as part of childhood---instead of her time with books about the lives of people. After nearly three years out of family life, she also needs uninterrupted time to readjust to being part of our lives again without the school homework of challenging grades. Her return to school should not be this term but the next term that starts after the Christmas and New Year holidays."

All family agreed with Linda. All ignored Nina's preference to skip grades and return to school for the current term. There was four months before the next term that started in January. The school principal accepted the decision of Nina's parents: She would return to school after New Year and be fixed in the fifth grade.

All the preliminary work about Nina that Linda wanted was accomplished. Linda knew that fifth graders changed classrooms with a different teacher for each of their studies. Linda was now ready to use her copies of audited tax returns to use Jean's family. Jean's Aunt Maria was a teacher with seniority in the school attended by children of Michael and Jean and children of divorced Millie. Millie's eldest son Rick would graduate eighth grade before the Christmas and New Year holidays recess.

Linda used Jean's sister Lucy to have their Aunt Maria use lunchroom talk with other eighth grade teachers for their help to encourage Rick to run-away from home. This would free Linda's daughter Lynn of duty to marry Rick, free Linda's sons of duty to be big brothers for him, and free their family of having to make Rick part of their restaurant business. All would be accomplished with *clean hands* for Linda and her family.

Linda had other uses of Jean's family in these months before Nina's return to school. Lucy was to have her Aunt Maria use lunchroom talk with kindergarten teachers worried about if they'd have fifteen-year-old Carlos in their class for the next term. Aunt Maria was to make the teachers see a way to be free from worry if Carlos was put into fifth grade where children begin to change classes and have different teachers for different studies. In this way, no one teacher would have him in class for the whole school day. Kindergarten teachers should be encouraged to join each other to suggest this to the school principal. Time would be needed for paperwork to transfer Carlos and to prepare fifth grade teachers who all knew the past ten year's history about him. The change would be start in January. Fifth grade teachers were told that Carlos' sixteenth birthday is at the end of June and none would have him in their classroom for more than one term---for only a few months that is interrupted with school closure for the Spring break. After Carlos' birthday, he would be forbidden back on school premises based on behavior since his start in this school with kindergarten.

Work for this change included that Aunt Maria was to learn what fifth grade homeroom Nina would be put into. When known, Aunt Maria's continued work was to have Carlos and Nina assigned to the same homeroom. Nina's lost memory about family life made her also forget what she knew about Carlos; only she would not know that Carlos didn't belong in fifth grade.

* * * * * * * * * * * *

Different family made Michael and Jean unable to get his other children to help Nina relearn the way to and from school while Linda required Lucy to walk Nina to and from school.

Thirteen-year-old Lewis told his father, "I'm not going to be a babysitter for an eleven-and-a-half-year-old sister. Tests proved she has the IQ of a twenty-one-year-old! She should be able to figure out the way to and from school when you draw a map for her to follow. I don't care about someone who has hurt my life. She's to blame for our changed lives. I miss having children at school refer to me as the boy with rich parents. I miss our large family gatherings with a lot of cousins to play with."

Seven-year-old Donald was brief when he told his father, "I don't want to look or feel like a baby who needs to be watched or helped by an older sister."

Ten-year-old Tricia's words were the loudest: "I was born with a readymade sister. I didn't know how different life could be without her until after her accident. I don't care what she's suffered, how tough it's been for her, or how alone she's been for the past three years. Only my life matters! No one can prove I'm guilty of any bad or wrong and *who* could do it won't do it without risks! All adult family said the accident must be punished. All family share the blames for her abandonment and isolation. I owe nothing to anyone!

"I'm still the same person I was before she was taken back. I didn't change my mind like other family have done. Everyone now falls all over her. It's as if I don't exist or matter anymore. Not even Nina could figure out why she gets so much attention now that she looks normal when fully clothed with hemlines below her knees to hide the scars above her knees.

"Tests prove she has the brains to find her own way to and from school with a map you could give her to follow until she knows the way. I also won't give up my friends and routine for her like I'm being asked to do for her needs. She makes her own friends like all children new to the school do. I don't care if sisters are to be each other's friends who care about and help each other. I want to pick my friends and not have one forced upon me. I decide when I want a new friend and who it would be. Having rich parents used to let me pick and choose friends but now I can only choose from who wants my friendship. Having rich parents would have let me pick and choose who I married but now I can only count on my good looks and nice shape for this. I don't like being the poor family among rich families. I don't like wearing hand-me-down clothes from the welfare system, nor how our neighbor families and school children react to it.

"I won't regret not wanting a sister back in life. I've done okay without her for the past three years. I'll marry when older. I'll have the company of my husband, our children, and the friends we make. I'll have a full life and won't think about if I do or don't have a sister.

"Her survival hurt our lives. Taking her back upsets everything and everyone. I'm used to not having to compete with an older sister. I liked being the only girl for my brothers. I liked the special treatment and attention as our family's only girl. I liked having a private bedroom that no one entered without my permission, and I liked having the big bed for only me."

Michael's voice was now loud enough to hears his firm words to Tricia, "Have you finished what you want to say?"

"No! Nuns told our mother that what was done would be a permanent record in the hospital because it was so rare. Even if family could someday remove or change that record, school records with her lost time are permanent unless someone could also change that. My brothers and I suffer being in the same school before and after her accident. She'll be required to wear certain clothes for gym class that would show some of her scars. Questions about it are natural and lead to more questions. Things we said in school when she was abandoned are now lies. Only she has no reason to lie. She has scars on her body as proof of very serious injuries that could further make our lies unbelievable.

"My brother Lewis will be the first to graduate from this school and be free of questions about her. Meanwhile my younger brothers and I remain in the school with her for the continued questions of school children about her different ways and the scars on her body. Gossip among children in school mean that children of all grade levels know things about Nina. When she has graduated this school's eighth grade, it won't mean that our continued time in it would free us of talk about her. Schoolteachers could also hurt our continuance in the school. Books she read in the two years alone at home helped her to have a high IQ and high marks. Our lives would be troubled when my brothers and I follow her to teachers she had. It would be the same trouble as it was for our cousin Nancy when she followed her two sisters with high IQs and high school marks. It wouldn't matter that it's always been hard work for me to have whatever marks I get. Teachers would expect the same work and grades from me that my sister had. Pressure for this could only make it harder for me to get even the passing marks I always have."

More than once, Michael's voice was firm when he interrupted Tricia. "Please stop the loud talk. All you've loudly said could be heard by Nina in her bedroom above us."

"I don't know why you worry that she could hear what I say. She learned to live with the truth. Abandonment made her understand that no family cared about her. She dealt with rejection and abuse while bedridden for the year she was in the hospital. She felt it more when back here and no family visited her---no family was company for her in the private room you made for her. She said that children in the big hospital room with her and their parents couldn't be stopped from all said and done that hurt her in different ways. What I say and do doesn't make her suffer more than what she has already experienced!"

Michael drew a map that showed Nina the way to and from school. On her first walk to school with an open book in her hand, she was surprised to hear Aunt Lucy's voice behind her: "May I be company for your trip to school?"

"Why do you want to do this?"

"I have the time and the inclination. You could get hurt if you read while walking to and from school. You could stop reading to cross the street but not all automobile drivers slow down at street corners even when there is a STOP sign. Some drivers concentrate on turning the corner without a look to see if a pedestrian is crossing the street." Niece and aunt walked side by side to the school with little conversation after that.

When on school grounds, Aunt Lucy said, "I'll come back to this same spot before school ends today to be company for your walk back home."

While Nina was in the school playground waiting for the bell to start classes, Carlos was telling Maude, "Your family owes for the divorce of my parents. They owe for the court ordered money my mother hasn't received before or after your aunt and my father ran off together."

In a stressed voice, Maude replied, "No one breaks a marriage that's already broken. Men seek other women when unhappy at home. No one owes for the choices and decisions of others. God and America give everyone free will for their own decisions and choices. No one owns another person's life. I don't know where your father is. Neither I nor my family owe anything to you or your mother. You and your mother troubled your own lives."

"Your family owes for the divorce of my parents. Your aunt made it happen when she stole my father from my mother. After your aunt and my father ran off together, your lawyer uncle didn't help to find them to enforce the court ordered money for my mother. This adds to why your family owes for the troubled lives of my mother and her children."

"No one owes for the debts and wrongs of others. Teachers have said that some illiterates are like animals or uncivilized savages. My family lives in civilized ways. A lawyer as part of our family is proof that we are educated and know right from wrong. People make their own way in life. You and your mother want people to better your lives as a debt instead of with your own work. Stop bothering me. Stop trying to ruin my life. Bother someone else and ruin that person's life.!" Maude didn't go to the assigned classroom. She went to the school office where she told the staff what happed in the school playground. The school principal said nothing could be done because he didn't physically harm her in any way. She then left this school's premises without return to it.

At the school day's end, Aunt Lucy was where Nina was to find her. On the walk to Nina's home, Aunt Lucy asked, "How was your first day in school?" Nina told her about the battle between two students in the school playground. Also, that she saw the girl leave school grounds before the school bell for the start of classes.

Nina didn't ask the question that Aunt Lucy explained: "The girl didn't have to spend one day in that school after none of its staff could help her. The school could do nothing because the boy didn't physically touch or harm her. You heard the girl say she has an uncle who is a lawyer. He would use legal loopholes for her immediate transferred to a different school since she lives on the boarder of two school districts. It would be a quick end of that boy's harassment for her."

Lewis was part of the playground crowd that surrounded the battle between Carlos and Maude. Lewis reported the battle between Carlos and Maude to Linda as was her rule---and to his close ties with their cousin Nancy. Family recorded what people said and did to make them someday *eat words and ways;* family activities would later make Maude *eat words and ways* no matter how long it took.

More Duty Marriage Battles

Easter in March was unusually early as was its comfortably good outdoor temperature. Business doors of these families were closed. A family picnic was held in the nearby public park but Lance, Julie and their young son again did not join them. Bertha, Wayne and their three daughters stayed close to each other at the picnic. Their voices became loud enough to be heard by all family as they battled about who would be *his* [Carlos'] bride---and Linda's rules for duty.

Eighteen-year-old Leslie was five feet three inches tall with a good teenage figure, black wavy hair, brown eyes, and normal size lips. Her nose was only slightly larger than average noses, and more attractive than elder family. She was ready to graduate high school in June with plans to enter college in September for journalism studies.

Leslie's fifteen-year-old sister Paula would be in high school two more years before she graduated and began college for studies in television work. Paula was two inches shorter than Leslie and better looks than this older sister. Paula had very good facial complexion, a good figure, black wavy hair, normal size lips, brown eyes and nose only slightly larger than average noses. Paula used her singing talent in the church choir and for family weddings. She donated her singing talent to charity work for which she made her own special clothes.

Their twelve-year-old sister Nancy was a grade school student with passing marks but a determination to have a high school diploma. Unlike two older sisters, Nancy had no interest in college. She had the misfortune of unappealing looks and shape that forever troubled her life.

As first in line for duty to be Carlos' bride, Leslie voiced strong feelings about this and a variety of family issues: "Womenfolk are not chattels or the property of their father or husband. Fathers and husbands should not treat their womenfolk as if concubines, servants, or slaves. Money shouldn't be used to force obedience, respect, or control. It's not right that fathers refer to their children as if only theirs when children equally belong to the mother but more than to the father. A child grows within the mother's body for nine months before birth. The infant's flesh and blood are from its mother. I don't want to buy a husband and don't want to support one. I don't want to feel like or be viewed as a cradle snatcher with husband three years younger than I am. Married couples should be intellectual equals. It's okay for a husband to have more brains and ambition than his wife, but not the other way around. An illiterate husband is an insult and burden. There's no respect for a husband who doesn't provide for his wife and children.

"We've been introduced to divorce and abandonment that left mother and children without the needed court ordered alimony and child support. Divorce is proof that no one owns anyone. It helps to prove that women need a good education to support selves with honest and good paying work, whether they do or don't marry. It could protect the woman against a husband who mistreats her, uses money to control her, or used any way to keep her in a bad marriage. A womanizer insults his wife and puts her health at risk.

It's not a compliment when a husband leaves his wife for another woman. Chances are high that he'd do the same to the next woman who married him."

Linda interrupted, "Who will pay for such an education?"

"I'll pay for my degree in journalism if my rich parents refuse. I could do the same as students who take wage paying work to pay for their higher education. On another issue that doesn't need to be put into spoken words, loving and caring adult family don't deliberately hurt their growing children in any way. Loving and caring family also don't make their growing children unknowingly guilty of doing it. Adult family should not give anyone chances to hurt their own with abandonment for any reason nor for any amount of time."

Paula voiced her feelings in a quieter voice and with less spoken words than Leslie. "I agree with all that my sister said without repeating it. I add that I want to love and respect who I marry. I value and want self-respect."

Linda temporarily lost self-control after hearing all said by Leslie and Paula. Linda's arms waved above and around her head as she yelled: *"No love! No like! All that matters are duty to family. Learn to like and respect the husband after the wedding day.* High school is already too much education for girls. It gives them too many ideas that hurt family life. A man's delicate ego is hurt if his wife is more educated than he is, or if she earns more money than he does. Husbands must not lose their place as head of their home."

Refusals of Leslie and Paula to be Carlos' bride made their sister Nancy last in line for it. Linda decided that Leslie and Paula were now available to marry her sons,

Chester and Gino but both sisters refused. Leslie and Paula used the same words and loud voices with their rejection to being brides of Chester and Gino, *"NO! Such a marriage would be incest!"*

Linda said, "Money stays with money! You two sisters and my sons are third cousins. The church said blood third cousins could marry each other. Did you ever think that you could marry a blood tie and not know it?"

Leslie said, "I won't marry my own type and kind. I don't like how our menfolk treat a wife. Jewish men make the best husbands and there's no worry about having the same blood."

Leslie's voice was louder when she unexpectedly asked Linda: "Who died and made you a queen? What qualified you for the honor of being our matriarch?" Linda made no verbal response and turned to face Nancy who now voiced her feelings to parents and to Linda.

"I have no younger sister to pass this duty to. I don't like being tagged last in line to marry that boy to pay for my uncle's bride. Life got mixed up when Aunt Linda refused to let Uncle Lance have the next bride in line [Lucy]. The bride [Julie] for Uncle Lance was to free the other one [Lucy] to marry Aunt Linda's son. It's not our fault that she [Lucy] still refused to marry him even after Uncle Lance's wedding.

"Like my sister, I refer to other issues. Punishment for divorce didn't have to leave the mother with young children without the needed money. It's not fair to give us the trouble that others caused as punishment. They had plenty of their own for duty marriages to make amends for the damages they arranged. They didn't have to pass it for us to clean their dirty laundry.

"I didn't ask to be born nor forced my parents to keep me. I had nothing to do with adult family troubles. I may be family's ugly duckling and get only passing school marks, but these are not good reasons to further destroy my life with duty to marry that boy. He's nearly sixteen years old and the school hasn't been able to teach him to read, write, or civilized life. No teacher could get him to leave his mother to do something with life as his older brother did.

"No one in school could be bought to befriend him. Parents of the students complain to the school that he's a bad influence and warn their children to avoid him. Our close cousins in the same school with him have nothing to do with that boy. Except for our cousins in the same school with him, he hasn't met us to know what we look like and the businesses we own. He's the barrel's bottom. An illiterate is an insult and burden for even someone with only passing school marks but would be a big insult for someone with good brains, good looks and figure."

Wayne pleaded with his daughter Nancy. "If you marry him, he'll replace the only son your mother and I had but died while an infant. If you marry this boy, he'd become part of our tavern business that would pass to you and him when your parents retire or our lives end."

"No one that I marry could replace the son that my parents lost. I don't want to spend life working side by side in business with a husband like my mother does. I don't care if my parents give me the tavern if I marry that boy because it gives who and what I don't want."

Linda interrupted, "Nancy is a born scrapper".

Nancy continued to verbally unwind. "I had to learn how to defend myself. I have no brothers for this like some girls. Children in school, some teachers and other adults make fun of my manly looks, my big bones and chunky shape, my oversized breasts, and clumsy ways. Some children and adults label me a *monkey*. Some of them stare at me while they make motions that resemble monkeys. I could let it wear me down or fight. I often wonder how some people would feel if something made them suffer as I do.

"I can't change how I was born or how I grow. God forgot about me when He made me different from other family and from most humans. Uncle Michael doesn't pick at how I am, but it feels the same when he talks about having *the most beautiful children among us*. He now adds boasts about the school tested high intelligence of one daughter. Everything about his children makes me and Aunt Linda's daughter Lynn feel inferior and worsens our jealousy.

"My sister Leslie has brains and ambition. My sister Paula has the same but also a personality that draws people to her without even trying. Paula has very good complexion and a winning smile with nice teeth. She has singing and piano talents. She designs and makes the special beautiful clothes she wears when she donates her talents to family weddings and to fund-raising charities. Paula has a lot of good in her favor and can afford to be like she is. All about Paula makes me as jealous of her as I am about Uncle Michael's daughters. Maybe someday there would be something in my life to make Paula and the others jealous of me."

Linda's voice softened. "Nancy creates new ideas. Nothing is owed for the bride [Julie]. Lance treats her right, she shares property with him, and doesn't work in a business with her husband as Bertha and I do. *Punishment for divorce continues! Their battles continue!"*

Linda was not too far away from the arguments when Nina asked her, "Why so much argument about who marries who?"

Linda said, "It's the way of growing girls. No one could predict their future, but every girl wants to be a bride."

"Marriage has not been on *my* mind. All family knows that I want to be a nun when old enough to enter the convent. As my godmother, I have another question for you: *Why didn't you do anything for me when I was in the hospital?* Why didn't you visit me in the hospital or when I continued to recover at home? Why did all family make me look and feel so unwanted when I needed them all so much?"

"Godparents have no duty when biological parents are alive and physically able to be employed to provide for their family. Some of your adult family spend long hours every day in their business. Some of your adult family are employed most days in a week. Our families have growing children in school with school homework. In addition to this, our children of all ages also help in the business of their parents. All this leaves little if any time for anything else."

Linda's voice and manner suddenly became authoritative: "You were in good hands. You did a service. The church owed! Everyone didn't have to suffer for one person. Forgive! Forget! That's all in the past! Life goes on."

"What service did I do? The church owed for what? How could anyone forget what becomes permanent parts of life, like my scars and the damaged shape of my body?"

"They owed! No more questions! That part of your life fades out of mind with the years."

Linda rushed from Nina back to Bertha, Wayne and their three daughters. With an excited voice, Linda told them, *"We have a dummy! Waste not, want not!"*

Nina heard those words and asked went to her father to ask, "What's a dummy?"

Michael also heard Linda's words, and spoke to Nina with more than one concern. "A dummy is like a doll but has movable parts. Ventriloquists are people who keep closed lips as they move body parts and lips of a dummy to make it look like the dummy spoke. I'll get back to you for more of your questions. I must now handle something while it's still an open subject."

Michael silently recalled what Nina told him Thanksgiving Day about three years ago. From behind the bathroom closed door, Nina then heard Bertha and Linda plan to punish a braggart. He now left Nina and headed straight to Linda where he spoke to her in a strong angry voice that Nina heard: *"This is not a joke!* Your games and tricks made this happen!"

"I had nothing to do with why the accident happened. No one could have predicted or even imagined such a thing. Only one person is still to blame for not keeping her promise to help you with the children on the accident night. No one pointed a gun at you for who and what was used to save and then to reclaim the child's life. You had free will to accept or reject the plans that I arranged for you.

"All that is in the past. We now need a way to put The Family back together as a whole. Smart people make use of the readied mold for abuse, inability to fight for self and acceptance of only life's barest necessities. Waste not, want not! You could now make amends for what was bragged about during the wedding. It would be a way to say *thank you* for the help that saved the child's life. It would be a way to say *thank you* for the help to safely reclaim the child's life. The unwanted duty marriage could put the beautiful and highly intelligent with the needy. The groom [Carlos] would have a bride already molded to accept whatever life would hold instead of a bride that matched his battling trait.

"Lucy must be part of what's needed to work free will. She needs a chance to make amends for her wrong on the night of the accident."

Michael said, "It *will* happen. Priority must be for what keeps The Family together." After he accepted Linda's plan, she telephoned Lance and Julie to inform them about the changed bride for Carlos---and they accepted the change.

Michael's family were back in their apartment where Nina returned to the front porch private bedroom built for her. Michael told Jean and their children what Linda offered and he accepted. Nina heard the loud laughter of siblings and parents in the far-off kitchen. She called for her father whom she asked, "What was so funny that I could hear laughter from the far-off kitchen to where I am?"

Michael told her, "I can't remember what made us all laugh. It was whatever broke the seriousness of school homework for your sister and brothers. I know that laughter helped us all to relax but can't recall what did it."

Lewis listened to what Aunt Linda and Aunt Bertha asked him to do and how it benefited him: "Help us to pass your cousin Nancy's marriage duty. She and Carlos are fighting people who could hurt each other in many ways if married to each other. A bride for Carlos is to end his trouble making ways that hurt the lives of his father's family and family of the woman who ran off with his divorced father. A bride for Carlos is needed for the promise your Uncle Lance made to his wife [Julie] and her family, and lawyer connected to Julie's family.

"Lewis, you would gain at least two benefits with help to accomplish the transfer. For one, it could free you of punishment for your refusal to marry Carlos' sister. Another benefit is that Carlos would no longer chase you in school after his interests are directed to Nina."

Carlos strongly resembled gangsters seen in motion pictures. He was five feet two inches tall with a firm body, thick black wavy hair, brown eyes, full lips, and a long broad nose. Carlos began to chase Lewis when on school grounds after he learned that his Aunt Julie married Lewis' Uncle Lance to make them cousins without blood ties. Another reason for Carlos to chase Lewis was that Lewis was arranged to be his future brother-in-law. All this also gave Carlos a reason to chase Lewis at school for some relief of his friendless life.

Lewis knew that passing Nancy's duty marriage freed her of punishments for rejecting it. Lewis didn't think to question how any family could speak on behalf of Uncle Lance who arranged the marriages for this generation. Nor did Lewis suspect silent punishment from his Aunt Bertha who silently continued to feel Lewis wasn't adequately punished three years ago when he pushed Nancy down a long flight of steps, laughed as she fell and laughed as she climbed back up. Aunt Bertha also silently and forever blamed that fall for why Nancy didn't have the same brains and ambition as her two older sisters.

Lewis had pictures of his sisters for the work he would do with Carlos in the school playground. Lewis knew which children could be bought for gang style activity in different parts of the school playground to frighten his sisters without physical harm. He was not concerned about the long-term effects for his frightened sisters. In the school playground on the next school day, two separate groups of students became gangs that surrounded Nina and Tricia. Each sister reported what happened to school staff who said nothing could be done because the girls were not physically harmed. Their parents could do nothing to change the decisions of the school staff. When all this was accomplished, the door was open for Lewis to approach Carlos.

When Lewis approached Carlos for help, Carlos asked, "Why should I help with your duty as their brother? What's in it for me?"

"You know that you and I became cousins without blood ties when my Uncle Lance and your Aunt Julie married each other. My sisters use different parts of the school to get to and from their classes. I can't be in both places at the same time to watch and protect each of my sisters. They need protection for time before the school bell signaled the start of morning and afternoon classes and during mid-day lunch breaks that many students take in the school playground.

"Nina is the one you should watch because she is one and one-half years closer to marriage age than my other sister. Your time to protect Nina could make her your bride and make many boys jealous of you. She has good looks, a nice shape and highly intelligent. When married, her school tested good brains could earn good wages to support both of you. With this added benefit, you could use marriage to become a business owner who doesn't punch an employer's time clock."

When Lewis won Carlos' interest in Nina, Nancy was freed of this duty marriage. This work tightened the cousin bonds of Lewis and Nancy that Tricia joined. These three spent much time together concentrating on activities that keep Carlos and Nina together. It helped to assure Tricia she would not be passed this duty marriage as the youngest and last in line for it. Also, for Lewis to not have Tricia forever blame him for having passed the duty if tricks didn't keep it with Nina. Family referred to the bonds of Lewis, Tricia and Nancy as *The Three Musketeers*.

Tricia knew about Aunt Lucy's severe guilt and blames for the accident night. Tricia was careful to never give even a hint to her that she [Tricia] could be blamed and suffer such pain instead. Tricia also knew Aunt Lucy's current duty to make amends for the accident night was to make Nina connect with Carlos.

Aunt Lucy was twenty years old, never employed nor sought employment. Part of her work was to walk Nina to and from school. They were together on the way to school when Nina heard Aunt Lucy mumble, "This duty services the future my sister agreed to."

Nina asked, "What duty and how does it service the future?"

"It's something that can't be explained. Ignore what you heard me say then and any other

times when I can't explain what you hear me say. I often think aloud without realizing that my words could be overheard. We're now at the school building where you enter for homeroom. I'll be at these footsteps at the school day end to walk you back home." There was very little talk between aunt and niece when they left school grounds that day for the walk back to Nina's home.

On their next day's walk home from school, Aunt Lucy asked Nina, "How was school today?"

"The boy who fought with a girl in the school playground is in my homeroom class. Everyone avoids him in homeroom class as they do in the school playground. No one gives him any attention, not even a glance. I heard his name when he responded to the teacher's attendance call. His name is Carlos and he looks much older than all other students in our homeroom."

"Do you know why he could be older than other children in class? Do you feel sorry for how he's being treated? Paying attention to these things is part of the qualities needed when you become a nun to help people in need."

"I know only what I saw and heard between him and a girl in the school playground. It didn't make him likable. It makes me want to avoid him like everyone else does."

"But that wouldn't be a nun's way. You do remember what it was like when children in the hospital and their visitors treated you like an outcast. Wouldn't that experience make you feel sorry for him?"

"My experiences were very different from how things are about him. This boy looks healthy, moves and talks without problems. He's the only student in this school who smokes cigarettes in the playground and also known to smoke in the boys' bathroom. He looks and acts like mean gangsters in movie films. His stares at me in homeroom and in the school playground. He frightens me."

"But you understand how he feels as an outcast. Isn't that enough to feel sorry for him instead of frightened? And the Bible says God tells us to not be afraid."

"I understand how he might feel as an outcast but don't know why absolutely all students avoid him at all times. Our homeroom teacher waits for his response to attendance call, but she doesn't talk to him or look at him after then---and he doesn't go to the teacher for anything."

"You remember how you felt when children in the hospital and their visitors refused to believe you. Being a friend for him would give you chances to hear his side of things. After that, you could choose to believe or not believe what he tells as was done to you in the hospital."

"Aunt Lucy, he is without friends in school but probably has a family at home that lets him know he is *never* alone in life. That's different from my being alone for most of three years from the night of my accident to being back in school. Aside from all that, I'm not yet a nun and girls and boys aren't each other's friend. I don't want anyone to think he's my boyfriend. Until I become a nun, I want to make friends with girls. I want to learn and do the safe things done by girls of my age."

"Nina, it's not rare for boys and girls to be each other's friend. Boys and girls who are neighbors become friends. Being one person's friend doesn't mean you couldn't have other friends. Growing children have a variety of interests shared with different friends. Aside from that, philanthropy is another way to look at things. A philanthropist is a wealthy person whose money helps people to get back on their feet without having to repay the money. After that is accomplished, the philanthropist leaves the person to go on with life without more help."

"I still don't want him as a friend. The way he harassed the girl in the school playground lets me believe what she told him---that he and his mother expect people to better their lives instead of doing it themselves. It doesn't sound like even a philanthropist would be able to help this boy. I witnessed the school playground battle; it wasn't gossip that reached me. His behavior made me believe he is mean and aims to win whatever wanted as if entitled to it. Nothing proved or indicated that he has used his time and energy to build a bettered life. I'm home now. Thanks for the company Aunt Lucy."

Nina entered the kitchen behind the family business when Michael asked her, "How was school today?" Nina told him the same things she told Aunt Lucy, and what Aunt Lucy said.

Michael said, "Let's talk more about this after supper. We can walk alone together in the outside fresh air where no one interrupts us." During the walk, Michael offered a new approach for Nina to connect with Carlos: "As Aunt Lucy said, philanthropists are rich people whose money helps people without monetary repayment. There are also people who are known as Good Samaritans. These people use their time and energy to help people and expect nor more return than a thank you for their help. You're alive today due to the good deeds of hospital nuns and priests. What was done for you was a combination of philanthropy and Good Samaritan work. Good Samaritans do what's needed and then leave the person to go on with life as done by philanthropists. Good Samaritans also do not expect their good deeds to form a lifetime attachment with the person who was helped. It's just good deeds. Being a friend for the boy in need fits into your plans to be a nun with work to help all who are in need. Being a friend is being a friend when needed; it's being a Good Samaritan. In rare situations, a deeper relationship sometimes develops between the Good Samaritan and the person helped."

"As a nun I'd be in clothes they wear. Who I helped would know it is part of my duty as a nun, but I'm not yet wearing nun's clothes!"

"Here's another way to look at help for a friendless person. You want friends. You can't make friends unless you could be a friend. Making friends with this boy is a way to show other children you could be a friend. I'm thinking out loud of a reason for you and this boy to get to know each other. He might have a reason to walk you home from school and you allow him to walk you home."

The next day in the school playground before the bell rang for classes, Lewis told Carlos how to use classroom time for a reason to walk Nina home from school. In the homeroom class, Carlos had a button in his opened hand when he went to where Nina was seated: "Would you sew this button back to my jacket? I don't know how it fell off. My mother gives me needle and thread to carry for if this happened away from home, but it never happened before now. You now have sewing classes; I never learned how to use needle and thread or to sew anything."

Nina recalled her father's talk about Good Samaritans and a way for other children to see her as a friend. She sewed the button on Carlos' jacket while in homeroom. Nina didn't think this could become gossip and travel into other classes. Nor did she think it would be viewed as Carlos' claim of her and her acceptance of a relationship with him.

At the school day's end, Nina was surprised to see Carlos instead of Aunt Lucy at the school building footsteps to walk her home. Carlos said, "I thought that if you let me walk you home and carry your books it would be a way to thank you for sewing the button on my jacket. I didn't want my mother to see it off my jacket. I'd like you to meet my mother if your parents let me to take you to our home. After that, I'd walk you home before your family's mealtime."

Nina didn't respond to Carlos about meeting his mother. "I'm home now, Carlos. Thank you for walking me here." Nina rushed from him into the kitchen behind the business of her parents. Once inside, Michael again asked her the same question he asked at the end of each school day: "Did anything new or different happen in school today?"

Nina explained about Carlos in homeroom and the walk to her home. Michael said, "Let him take you to meet his mother. Let him show off to his sister and mother that he finally made a friend at school."

Nina followed her father's suggestion for Carlos to take her to meet his mother to show he finally had a friend. Carlos, his sister and their mother Millie lived in a second-floor apartment of a multiple family tenement building. The hallway was filled with smells of different ethnic food. Millie was a short chubby woman with black hair, brown eyes, full sized lips, and nose a little larger than average women. Introductions were upon entering the apartment and as they headed to the kitchen where cookies and milk were on the table. Instead of getting to know Nina, Millie began a monologue about her life from wedding day to the present without pauses:

"My husband's adultery was an *insult*. It was *compounded with injury* when he and his mistress ran away and not found for the court ordered alimony and child support. He *abandoned our innocent young children*. The church gives little help to a divorced woman with young children. The tax funded court system and probation office didn't prove they searched for my ex-husband to enforce the court ordered money. It forced me to work outside our home. Taxes and union dues deducted from my wages didn't leave enough to properly provide for my growing children. I have a right to expect *returns* for the taxes I'm required to pay.

"Taxes taken from my earnings include funds for the school system; its teachers became the source for some *returns*. When Carlos began kindergarten, he obeyed my instructions and understood it was a *secret* between only him and me. Carlos was to do whatever made a teacher keep him after school, so I wouldn't worry about him while at wage paying work. He's been the most affected by the loss of his father and I worried that he'd get into trouble. Carlos was attached to his older brother and again hurt when his brother recently ran away from home.

"When Carlos was very young, he couldn't understand that our troubled lives were arranged to punish my divorce; he understood it as he grew older and saw other families in this building with very little troubled lives. When my firstborn son ran away from home, it was the *straw that broke the camel's back*. It left only Carlos for when my bad health or old age ended my employment years. Carlos wouldn't be able to care for me when that time comes unless his life was bettered before then."

Nina silently reacted to much but put verbalized none to Millie. Nina looked at a clock on the kitchen wall and told Carlos and his mother it was near to her family's mealtime. With the excuse of not being hungry, Nina didn't drink the milk or eat any of the cookies, but thanked Carlos' mother for it as they said *goodbye* to each other. Carlos walked Nina to her home. Nina entered the big kitchen behind her parents' business and saw Aunt Lucy there again. Michael enthusiastically asked Nina, "How was your visit with Carlos' mother? Did you and she talk much with each other? Did she have cookies and milk ready for you? Was she nice to you? Did you like her?"

"His mother had cookies and milk waiting on her kitchen table but I didn't take any of it. I was very uncomfortable with her. We didn't share conversation. His mother talked non-stop while I was there. She talked a lot, a lot in detail about her life from her wedding day into her divorce and being cheated of court ordered alimony and child support. She said her runaway husband abandoned his children but I didn't tell her that she nor her children know what being abandoned means as I know it. She said the church was no help for divorced women with young children. I don't understand why she told me about life for her and her children. Maybe she needed someone to talk with about their lives, but it doesn't fit right to have chosen an eleven-year-old for it."

Lucy interrupted. "Carlos, his brother and sister were never abandoned. They always had each other and their mother. While the church doesn't approve of divorce, it allows children of divorced parents to remain part of the church and receive all of its religious sacraments."

Nina continued. "She talked about her runaway son and that it left her only Carlos for when she is no longer employed and for her old age. She talked about having encouraged Carlos to do whatever made a teacher punish him with detention after a school day's end. She didn't show even a slightest interest in his educational needs nor any interest in my plans for life."

Lucy again interrupted. "His mother falls into the group of parents without concern for their children's future. That type ignores a child's need for education to do something with life and more important for boys who grow to be adults to provide for a wife and their children."

Michael said nothing for or against what Lucy said.

On Sunday thereafter when businesses were closed to the public, Linda called for a family picnic in a nearby park. Lance, Julie and son again didn't join them. Jean's sister Lucy again made herself part of this gathering as if natural parts of Michael and Jean's family. Lucy preferred to know things firsthand and not a report about it. Lewis, Tricia, and their cousin Nancy skipped around Nina as they sang the song *Ring 'round The Rosie*. They laughed as they took turns to tap Nina's shoulder as they said, *"Tag! You're it!"* and then ran away from her.

Michael saw Nina's look of '*what's this about*' and told her, "Lewis, Tricia and Nancy are like the Three Musketeers. What they now did is a game called Hide and Seek that you forgot. In this game, each person taps one person and then quickly hide with waits for the tapped person to find each of them for an end to the game."

In school the next day, Nina noticed that her homeroom teacher appeared calmer since she [Nina] allowed time for Carlos. Nina didn't know what other classes Carlo was assigned to or if he showed up in them. Nina couldn't know if gossip about Carlos'

interest in her traveled to also relax schoolteachers who expected him in their classroom.

During lunch break in the school playground, Carlos stood at a distance as he

watched Nina play with girls. A girl broke from group activity and looked toward Carlos

who stood smoking a cigarette as she asked Nina, "Why do you spend time with that

boy?"

"I'm doing a good deed. I'm being a Good Samaritan for him."

Girls in that group and some that surrounded them joined with each other. They

took turns to tell Nina, "That boy doesn't understand Good Samaritan work. He doesn't

even qualify for the fifth grade or any grade level above kindergarten. Didn't your

brother and sister tell you to avoid him like they do---like everyone at school avoids him

If they didn't tell you, any schoolteacher could tell you about that boy. You should let

more than one teacher tell you about him. Each teacher learned different things about him

or had different experiences with him in their class. Things about that boy are known

throughout the school. A girl recently transferred out of this school before her first day in

any class to get away from him. Your homeroom teacher is the first one to ask about him,

and then the teachers you have for different subjects. Just the mention of his name starts

all kind of talk."

Schoolteachers Inform Nina About Carlos

Throughout the years, kindergarten teachers gossiped in the lunchroom about Carlos to vent how his behavior hurt their classroom teaching abilities, hurt how much children learned in their classroom, and how much it emotionally and mentally hurt each teacher who had him in their class. Fifth grade teachers backed up and added to what each of them told Nina. They responded to Nina with similar words: "There's no quick way to tell you about Carlos, but it's important that you know his history in this school to help you decide about more of your time for him. If you come to school with bagged lunch as I do, we could talk privately in this classroom during tomorrow's lunch break."

"I'll be here tomorrow at lunch time with bagged lunch." Nina wasn't concerned about how Carlos would feel when he couldn't find her in the school playground during lunch break.

Some schoolteachers memorized the report they were permitted to view about the school representative's visit with Carlos' mother that a repeated for Nina: '*Time and energy were wasted except for what was learned and otherwise never known, suspected, or imagined by high minded people. Carlos' mother said her wages were reduced with taxes and knew that some of it went to the school system---that it gave her the right to use taxpayer money to scapegoat the school system, and to lengthen a teacher's workday.*

Nothing and no one would be able to undo damages to Carlos with his mother's uses of him from a young and tender age for her spite work. His character and personality are fixed. It's our belief that he and his mother would destroy whoever might risk thinking they could do more or better than the school's trained staff.'

Nina's homeroom teacher said, "Gossip about Carlos among teachers in our lunchroom was routine. Talks were about trouble with him in class from his first day in school onward. The first troubled time with him made school staff believe his behavior was due to the divorce of his parents. School staff later added his talk about being abandoned by his father. Another belief for his misbehavior was that his mother became employed and he lost the time they had together. Teachers also considered that he heard hurtful gossip by children in the playground about him, his mother and runaway father that didn't help him to forget his painful life. Teachers were also concerned about Carlos' future after his brother ran away."

From another teacher: "Fifteen-year-old Carlos would soon be sixteen years old without an education or skill for wage paying work to help his mother's money needs, to support self, and when he becomes the provider of wife and children. Representatives of the school were assigned to discuss Carlos' school history with his mother and honored her demands for the meeting: (1) his mother was not to lose time from work for lost income, and (2) and the meeting was to be in her home for her to not have more time away from her children. The meeting let this school end guessing games about his misbehavior here. The meeting proved that feeling sorry for him helped nothing and no one; it reminded schoolteachers that our main and only duty is to educate children. The picture proved that no one should assume or presume answers to anyone's behavior.

However, *our teachers have since wondered how mother and son would feel if they became babysitters without the returns they expected.*"

Another teacher said, "Kindergarten teachers who had Carlos in her class needed to know the contents of the report about the meeting with his mother. They needed to rebuild confidence as teachers and as good humans. The report and suggestions from different teachers helped the decision to put Carlos in fifth grade where children go to different classes for different subjects. Before this change, results of the meeting with his mother were given to fifth grade teachers to calm them for the short time of day he'd be in each one's class---if he showed up in each class."

Another teacher said, "No teacher could get Carlos to read, write or live in civilized ways. Every school has its share of troubled or trouble-making children, but none like him. The most understanding, kind and patient of teachers became ill and needed medication for their nerves after a short time with him in class. Some teachers panicked before each new term with fear he'd be assigned to them. Some teachers transferred to other schools or took early retirement to avoid any possibility that Carlos would be put in their class.

"Carlos has been full of games and tricks that kept him in school after the end of every school day. Teachers have punished him with a dunce cap and made him stand faced to the classroom corner. He stayed there but turned to face the class and did whatever made students in class laugh. He didn't care that his behavior hurt the teacher's job or that it cheated him and other students of an education. All that has been experienced with him in this school for the past ten years would be unbelievable to who didn't witness it. Our school staff has predicted that he'd never change---not even if he someday learned to read and write.

"School staff have predicted he'd never be able to properly support himself and certainly never able to support a wife if lucky enough to have and keep one. Girls who sell their bodies don't even take a groom who is not able to provide or be the primary provider. And, this state's laws grant divorce to a wife whose husband doesn't provide for her. Nothing good could be said about him except that he has a healthy body and good teeth. This little bit of good proves bad when it means he might live longer than the average age with more years to hurt or destroy the lives of people that walk in his path."

Another teacher told Nina, "Carlos comes to school with a clean body, ironed clean clothes, and appears well fed but is a bad example in all other ways for our impressionable younger students. It's the school's duty to protect all students from bad influences but we've been unable to do anything about him. His mother has complained of not enough money to live in a better neighborhood, or to give her children the best food. Yet, she has given him money for his cigarette smoking habit from an early age. Neither Carlos nor his mother have used the law that allows fourteen-year-old children to quit school to help their family's money needs. He has never delivered newspapers to earn money like other boys do after school and weekends without the loss of formal education. Carlos knows nothing about responsibility for self or anyone else.

"Mother and son have said that amends were being made for the punishment with divorce. They claim it permitted them to pick and choose his future bride. They don't understand or believe that *amends are not made for what was deliberately punished*. With the inability of mother and son to live acceptable civilized lives, and if he is lucky to have a bride, God's help would be needed for the marriage to never produce children whose lives would be destroyed by him and his mother."

Yet another teacher said, "Carlos knows nothing about Good Samaritans and has no understanding of good deeds. He thinks that anything he and his mother do for anyone puts that person in debt to them. God's help is needed for who mother and son think owes them for even the smallest thing, and who doesn't satisfy them. Mother and son would punish that person and everyone in the person's life until sickened or destroyed like they are. They don't understand they must be grateful to whoever married him, and more grateful if she kept him. Whoever they choose to be his bride would suffer if she did or didn't marry him. The chosen bride's only chance to survive is to not give them total control with marriage.

"Mother and son have made it understood that they've out-witted highly educated people. Carlos wouldn't believe that his life is ruined with his mother's uses of him. He refused to leave his mother as his brother did for chances to do something with life. After the report about the visit with Carlos' mother, school staff considered legal proceedings for him to be placed in a residence for incorrigible children. Thought was also given to the fact that legal action at this late stage would take a long time before on the court calendar---and would likely happen after his sixteenth birthday when he's forced to quit school and thereafter stay off school grounds. The choice to put him in a fifth-grade homeroom helped to keep current kindergarten teachers from a full day with him in her classroom."

A week of talks from schoolteachers about Carlos and his mother made Nina recalled the overheard battles about duty marriage among her paternal cousins, Leslie, Paula and Nancy. But Nina had no proof those battles were about duty to marry Carlos.

At the end of each school day, Carlos was at the footsteps of the school building where Nina left for her walk home. She wondered if she should allow him to again carry her books and walk her home. Or, if she could come up with some excuse to prevent it today and forever after. On their past walks to Nina's home, Carlos repeatedly talked about what his mother, he and his sister suffered from before he began school into present time. He repeated that his mother was a good person who didn't deserve all that happened---and that he was the only son for her old age. Carlos never said anything about his loss of an education, nor how he would get an education or learn a skill for good wage paying work. He said nothing about his future as a responsible adult to provide for self and possible future with a wife and children. His ten years in kindergarten and lack of friends at school kept him from knowing about Nina's multiple traumatic experiences with burn injuries---or that it kept her out of school for more than three years.

Family made Nina a Good Samaritan for Carlos, but none helped her to know how to end the relationship she didn't like or want from the start. Classroom rules for assigned seats didn't allow Nina to move to another part of the homeroom where Carlos couldn't stare at her. A different homeroom without him wouldn't keep him away from staring at her in the school playground. The home of Nina's parents was on the boarder of two school districts. She aimed for a transfer to the other school, but it didn't happen. Family and school staff gave her different reasons why it couldn't happen for her as it did for the girl who transferred to another school to be free of harassment from Carlos.

Nina and Carlos began their walk from school to her home. She began with idle talk. "It's another nice day for walking. Spring is a good time of year."

"Yes, it is another nice day. Let me carry your books again until you are home."

"Thank you for the help Carlos, but not this time. I must get used to carrying books from school to my home as I do from home to school. You must think about when you also have to take books home for homework."

Carlos ignored response about books and homework for him when he said, "Going home with your books adds homework to the weight of your books. I could carry half of the books that you take home to lessen the extra weight for you. This way you'd still have company for trips home to the end of this school term."

"The weight of what I take home and take back to school is the same since it includes the homework both times."

"If that's what you want. But it won't change our being in the same homeroom and seeing each other in the school playground."

"Seeing each other in homeroom won't change but it would change in the school playground. I'm only eleven years old and need girlfriends for girly activities in the school playground. We're now where I live. Thank you for the company. Have a good weekend."

"You have a good weekend too, Nina."

As usual, Nina's return from school found her father waiting for her in the kitchen behind the family business. "How were things in school today, and the walk home with Carlos?"

Nina took a deep breath to hide her resentment and anger before she could speak calmly: "Nothing new. I've spent the week of lunch breaks with teachers for my different classes. What each teacher told me about Carlos made me think he was who my cousins battled against marrying before my return to school after my accident."

"How could it be the same boy? Those cousins don't go to the same school where you and he are. How could your cousins know things about that boy that teachers told you?"

"I saw Lewis and Tricia in the crowd around that boy and the girl he harassed in the school playground. Lewis and Tricia spend a lot of time with our cousin Nancy---and talks about all that happens is family gossip. The school's history about that boy is that no teacher could help or change him for better in the smallest way. All schoolteachers felt sure that his personality and character are permanent. This matches your favorite expression that *you can't change the spots on a leopard.* I have already suffered enough in my short life. I don't plan to worsen the rest of my life with him in it, not even as a Good Samaritan. Teachers said he's unable to understand Good Samaritan work---that he understands nothing about good deeds."

Aunt Lucy interrupted. "I'll again walk you to and from school every day. We can't help how this would make Carlos feel, but it should make him know he no longer walks you home."

"Thanks, Aunt Lucy."

Michael told Nina, "Put your books away and get some fresh air before meat time. There is nothing more to discuss now on this matter."

During the next day's walk to school, Aunt Lucy told Nina, "Carlos will know he won't walk you home after school when he sees me there for you. How do you think he might react?"

"I don't know but he frightens me. Before school starts and during lunch breaks, he stares at me while he smokes more than one cigarette in the thirty minutes break between morning and afternoon classes. I keep my back to where he stands or sits on the ground. I jump rope with the girls who helped me to learn about him when my own brothers and sister didn't do it."

"There's nothing to be frightened of. School staff protect children in the building and in its playground. The school could do nothing if Carlos doesn't touch or hurt you in physical ways. He's allowed on school grounds until his sixteenth birthday. I doubt he'd approach you while I am with you in the playground until the bell rings for the morning start of classes. I also doubt he'd approach you when he sees I'm waiting for you at the end of a school day."

"He frightens me even without a physical touch. I want him *forever out of my life. I'm anxious for the school summer break to be free of him.*"

* * * * * * * * * * * * *

Before school reopened for the winter term, Aunt Lucy told Nina, "Carlos enlisted into the navy and accepted with a lie about his age. The armed forces don't confirm an enlisted man's age when desperate for men during war time or when a war is expected. It's also most concerned with an applicant's strength and stamina than ability to read and write. Not all men in military are put into combat duty. Many of who are unable to read and write could be assigned to kitchen duty, to clean bathrooms and floors. The bright side is that enlistments are for seven years. During that time, his absence saves you and other people from his trouble-making ways."

Away with Part of the Past

Lewis' work for Carlos to concentrate on Nina freed him of being chased by Carlos in school. Nina was in the second half of sixth grade when Lewis graduated grammar school's eighth grade. Graduation freed Lewis of gossip among school children about Nina's three years absence and about his avoiding Nina when in school while younger siblings, Tricia, Donald and Jerry continued to experience these discomforts at school. Neighbors often asked Lewis, Tricia, Donald and Jerry why Nina wasn't seen with them.

Michael and Jean also felt the discomfort with neighborhood gossip. Gossip worsened when they couldn't show neighbors and business customers proof that Nina's medical care for burn injuries took them from great wealth to poverty: no cancelled checks or receipts on hospital stationary with paper age that showed dates and amounts paid to the hospital.

When Nina was to graduate grade school as valedictorian, Linda told her that no adult family would attend the graduation ceremony---there would be no family celebration of this special day---and she was to go on stage with the most unattractive homemade dress she [Nina] ever saw on anyone. Except for the dress, Nina accepted no family interest or happiness about the school honor of her because it was how family treated her older cousins Leslie and Paula who both graduated high school with high marks.

Paula and Linda's daughter Lynn were first cousins born in the same month of the same year. One of their differences was that Lynn's troubled school marks caused her to graduate elementary and high school at much later years than Paula or the average student. Linda's disapproval of high school education for family womenfolk changed for only her daughter Lynn. When Lynn graduated high school. Linda had a big party to celebrate it to which Michael, Jean and their children were not invited.

After Nina graduated grammar school's eighth grade, Michael and Jean moved their family into a different neighborhood from which Nina would enter junior high school. Younger Tricia, Donald and Jerry would enter a different grade school. In the family's new location, a neighborhood boy joined Nina for walks to the school where he also was a student. During their walks, they talked only about school issues and activities. Family insisted that Nina no longer walk to and from school with him. This made Nina recall similar family orders while in grammar school when she was told to not build a friendship with a certain girl. Both times were when Nina would have had friends with IQs near to hers. At that time when Nina and that girl aimed for friendship, Nina's father and Aunt Lucy said, "You need to spend time learning duties as a homemaker---not time with girls who have plans for more than marriage."

Nina's said, "I have sewing and cooking classes in school. When I'm in the convent, I'll be taught how they want things done. Nuns are educated people with a variety of duties who live together as a family with free time to socially connect with each other. When I was in grade school, you both wanted me to do good deeds for a friendless boy. Neither of you then allowed me to stay with who I intellectually connected and didn't need my help. Again, you both want me to not become friends with intellectual equals who don't need my help for anything."

Nina's father and Aunt Lucy said, "Who you want as friends may have high school marks as you do, but their skin color make it known they have parents of different races. People in our country part often react cruelly to children produced in mixed marriages. Before and now, we want to protect you from being subjected to the bad experiences directed to those children."

"It didn't feel like protection before or now. If I'm being protected from cruel ways of people, why did no family protect me from cruel things while I was bedridden for nearly a year in the hospital? Apart from that, I have a problem most people could not understand. Children my age in school make funny faces and noises when I give the right answers in class. One student in my class said my ability with quick right answers made other children feel unable to learn what was taught---made them feel inferior. My mother was told this would happen after tested for grade placement, but parents wouldn't allow my choice of more challenging work in higher grades. My sister and brothers spend no time with me. I don't understand why I was reclaimed instead of permitted to stay with the priests and nuns." Nina walked away and went back to hours reading books at home and during school lunch breaks.

Wedding of Rocco and Ella

Nina was fourteen years old when her maternal Uncle Rocco and Ella married

each other. It was a church wedding with an elaborately big wedding reception in a large

catering hall to which family of Nina's father were not invited.

Nina didn't get to know Ella or any of her family before this wedding. Since the

accident and before this wedding, Nina didn't see or hear from her maternal uncles or

extended family of her mother. The many lost years of contact made Nina unable to

recognize them in the church or in the wedding reception gathering---and none of them

approached Nina to remind her of their relationship in her life.

Nina went to one of many balconies in the reception hall where she looked down

at the crowd of people. Some guests were together at tables where they consumed food

and drink. It was obvious they were talking with each other when their hands and arms

were seen in motion. Musicians and a piano player provided continuous music to which

some adults danced with each other and some adults danced with the young children.

Uncle Rocco and Aunt Lucy were together when they approached Nina in the

balcony. Uncle Rocco asked, "Why did you separate yourself from everyone?"

"I'm not comfortable in a large crowd. I don't know most of the people here, not even family who didn't continue to be part of my life since my accident. I'm happy that you have someone to share life with. I'll never be married to a human but will share life serving God."

Aunt Lucy remained silent as Uncle Rocco said, "Nina, you're only fourteen years old. It's too young to be sure about the future. You'll marry just as all girls do when you're older."

"No. I'm different from other girls. I'm going to be a nun."

Aunt Lucy and Uncle Ralph left Nina alone on the balcony. They believed they were well out of hearing range when Nina heard Aunt Lucy's rushed words to Uncle Rocco: "You know Jean approved. Her decision to marry troubled our lives. Her approval of plans frees us. You also know I'd find ways to make the needed change in her future."

Nina didn't know when maternal Uncle Caesar and Eva married each other because her [Nina's] family weren't invited to their church wedding or wedding reception. After Nina's parents divorced, she was introduced to her new Aunt Eva when invited to the church baptismal of the first child (a son) that Uncle Caesar and wife produced. Eva's parents were born in Rome, Italy and she believed this made them more cultured than most other Italians and with above average good manners in addition to their good looks and good shape. The looks and ways of Nina's father didn't fit into all invited to this wedding.

Aunt Lucy and her parents were guests at this wedding while she was not yet connected to the groom that didn't fit into all invited.

Working Nina's Life

The weekend after Thanksgiving Day was little more than three months after Nina's birthday. For the first time and in the home of Nina's parents, there was a meeting of her mother's siblings Rocco, Sarah, Caesar, Lucy and their parents. Linda and none of Michael's blood family were invited. After the meal, Michael made the long walk to his business in a new location as his wife and her blood family expected. He worked at this business after wage paid employment, after family supper and on weekends. His time was mostly to clean and repair men's hats and the sale of men's accessories. Sometimes he molded unused fabric on hand and shaped it for hats that Jean later finished with linings, headbands, and brims.

Michael's departure left Jean with their children, her siblings and parents. Nina was surprised when seventeen-year-old Lewis and thirteen-year-old Tricia asked her to join them for a game in the back yard. Lewis gave Nina details about the game they called high-low jump: "Tricia would hold one end of this long piece of wood and I would hold the other end of it. You must jump over this piece of wood we would raise to new heights after each jump. The wood level starts at about one-foot above ground for the first jump. It is raised a foot after each jump until it's too high for you to jump over it to end your part of the game. You then hold the wood piece end that Tricia or I held to free one of us for our turn to jump over it."

"OK. I understand the game."

The game progressed to when the wood piece was three feet high. Nina was on the way to jump over it when it was suddenly raised higher so that her pelvic area hit hard on it. The wood piece was then dropped to the ground. Nina saw blood travel from her pelvic area down one of her legs. Silent Lewis and Tricia remained outdoors as frightened Nina rushed to their mother. Jean took Nina into the bathroom where she gave her a clean panty with folded clean cloth on its crutch and said, "Expect this every month for many years to come. What I'm now helping you to do is how to handle it each time this happens." Jean didn't tell Nina this began womanhood nor what it meant to be a woman in their family. Nina and her mother could not be certain that the flawed jump made this happen. Jean left Nina in the bathroom and went to the living room where the adult family remained seated.

Nina opened the bathroom door but not yet out of it when she heard her mother speak in a louder than usual voice: "*Finally*! Three months after turning fifteen but it finally happened!"

Immediately after that, Nina heard clapped hands with excited voices that said, "*Finally*! *Finally*! We could now move forward with life."

When Nina rejoined family in the kitchen, she asked, "What made everyone so happy? Why so much hand clapping?"

Everyone seemed to answer at the same time. "Family gatherings make us happy. It's just family talk. Clapped hands helped to wake grandpa who dozed off in the chair."

After the Christmas and New Year holidays, Nina would enter high school's tenth grade. It was also when her family moved to another part of the city---one that Aunt Lucy found for them. It was half a block from the bus that Michael would take to and from employment. It was around the corner from where Aunt Lucy lived with parents. The nearby bus began and ended its route across the street from the restaurant business of Linda and Paul whose son Chester still waited for Lucy to be his bride. Lucy's continued refusal of duty to marry Chester became gossip that kept bachelors from pursuit of her.

The apartment for Michael's family was in a six family, three level building. It was a railroad rooms style and much smaller than any place they lived in. This apartment was next to the one occupied by their landlords---a married couple who were opposites of each other in very clear ways: The wife was large boned, tall and well overweight; her husband was small boned, thin and short---his head fit under his wife's armpits. Their marriage produced children who grew to average heights and average bone structure. The husband was a very quiet man. His wife handled all family life and all things connected with the property.

The high school for Nina was four long blocks from where her family now lived. The grade school for Tricia, Donald and Jerry was two long blocks away from their home, in the opposite direction from the high school. Tricia would be in eighth grade for one year before she would be a high school freshman in ninth grade where Nina attended.

Two weeks after school began, Nina was in the bedroom shared with Tricia who was now two rooms away in the kitchen with their parents and Aunt Lucy. Tricia's voice was loud enough for Nina to hear: "It's bad enough that I still wear clothes that public assistance provides, but I'll soon be a freshman to follow my sister in the same high school. All the trouble left in the other school would again happen for me in high school. Teachers would expect my grades to be as good as hers. Scars on her thighs would show below the required gym suit for physical education and again get attention. The gym teacher and students would ask her about the scars, and she'd answer their questions. I'd be uncomfortable when later asked about things she told. I'd also be asked to explain why she behaves in weird ways and not like most girls. Gossip is as much a part of school life as it is in our family. Family nor I want people to know she was abandoned. People of all ages would be curious about why she was abandoned and how she felt when abandoned. They'd want to know how it affected me to have a sister, to suddenly lose her, and then suddenly have her back in life. Questions would go on into her having been reclaimed. Family isn't faced with these problems like I am. I said it before and repeat it now. Her survival hurt our lives. *Reclaiming her hurts everything and everyone!*"

Aunt Lucy said, "No problem. Tell everyone she lies—that she makes up stories!"

"It won't help as things are now and would continue. The scars on her legs aren't the only thing. The hospital nun told our mother that the fire destroyed the flesh to the bone of one hip and left a cavity on her torso. This would be proof she didn't lie about her life for people who see this part of her body. Aside from that, she's been made to be a Goody-Two-Shoe. Thinking type people would never believe that her type lies!"

"Stop worrying. I'm your aunt and baptismal godmother. Things could turn out in your favor. There's a whole year before the two of you are in the same school. She might become a high school dropout and you wouldn't have to explain anything to anyone in school."

Tricia's school hours were eight-thirty in the morning to three thirty in the afternoon. The overcrowded high school had split sessions. One session from eight in the morning to three in the afternoon. The other session from noon to five thirty in the evening. Some students from each session were in the same classes. Nina was assigned to the session from noon to five thirty. Different school schedules kept Nina and Tricia from too much contact with each other. Family's weekday evening meals were changed from six o'clock to five-thirty---the time when Nina's school day ended for her long walk home. The new schedule left Nina to have week night meals with only her father.

During a meal, Nina asked her father, "Why was family's supper time changed? I'm home a few minutes before our usual six o'clock time for all of us to eat together."

"Your sister and brothers are always uncomfortable with your prayers before every meal. Different school schedules and the changed time for supper frees them of it. There is no right or wrong. There's no good or bad. It's just that not everyone is as religious as life made you. Weekend meals are not always at fixed times because the five of you have different activities that don't make it possible to be together for all meals."

For an extra-curricular high school subject, Nina chose the Italian language. It was to help her speak with her grandmother who spoke minimal English after more than thirty-five years in America. Aunt Lucy showed excessive interest in Nina's Italian language teacher, students in Nina's class and in school activities she joined or planned to join.

"Aunt Lucy, why do you want to know everyone's name?"

"Names of students in school who become your friend open new conversations between you and me. The name of your teacher for Italian classes told her students that her husband is a doctor, and this is something different from who becomes your friend. You know your mother and I have an uncle and cousins who are doctors. Doctors get to know each other. People in the same profession are like a family; it's called a brotherhood. Your teacher's husband could be known to our family doctors with a likelihood they've been put them together for some medical issue. They also could have shared talk about your continued school progress after your accident.

"You said a girl named Cora is in your gymnasium class. I've heard that name only once before. I think she's a daughter of people who own a delicatessen and produce shop where I've shopped with grandma. The shop owner's wife and I chat with each other while her husband prepares our food order. Cora has an older sister and younger brother.

"Grandma, your mother and I also shop for fresh cut meat and grocery items in a store owned by two brothers and is closer to where you and I live. These two brothers, your mother and our brothers grew up with together. We did a lot together and were like cousins with them even though not blood connected."

* * * * * * * * * * * * *

In the month Nina began high school's tenth grade, Doctor Robert was discharged from military service. Aunt Lucy told everyone that he aimed to quickly build a private practice. He wanted his own fortune to be separate from the purse strings of his wife's family. His cousin Jenna and her husband owned the produce and grocery shop that Nina's mother and Aunt Lucy shopped at. Jenna and husband produced three children who were now nineteen-year-old Emma, sixteen-year-old Cora and fourteen-year-old Johnny. They lived together in the apartment behind their business. Nina passed their shop on her walks to and from school.

* * * * * * * * * * * *

Millie worked for her nineteen-year-old son Carlos to be discharge from the navy before the end of his enlisted time. He was never in combat duty. Grapevine gossip was that Millie sought his discharge with hysterical fear she'd lose *the only son left for her old age*. Continued gossip was that Millie didn't want Carlos to lose Nina for marriage as another punishment for her divorce. Carlos was discharged from the navy after only three years of his enlisted seven years.

* * * * * * * * * * * *

Michael's eldest niece (Nina's eldest cousin) was ready to leave family roots for a move across country with her journalism degree. Twenty-three-year-old Leslie paid her college costs without help from wealthy parents. Her departure was also against Linda's rule for none to stray from the fold. Before departure, Leslie visited fifteen-year-old cousin Nina to say goodbye and to advise her about ongoing life: "Get your education and run as far and as fast as possible away from here. You can't fight the odds. You can't beat the odds. Family ways will ruin your life."

Nina didn't understand this advice. Her father interrupted before she could ask Leslie to explain it: "Don't pay attention to Leslie. She's a rebel without a cause."

Leslie made no comment to what Uncle Michael said. She stood in front of all family there when she said, "If I even think my life was being arranged, all family should know and remember that *the pen is mightier than the sword!*" Leslie knew that one or more of who was there would repeat her words to other family.

Leslie now turned to speak to only Nina: "I'll write to you to find out how you're doing in school and what's happening in your life. I may be able to help in some way when you're ready for a move away from here. I'll write to you after I find a place to live with an address where you should write to me."

After many months passed, Nina didn't understand why she had no letters from Leslie. Mail was delivered in the early mornings. Nina's mother collected it from the building foyer's mailbox. Nina was always told there was no mail from Leslie for her. All family said they didn't hear from Leslie and didn't know where and how to contact her. Nina didn't imagine or suspect that family would prevent her and Leslie from continued contact with each other. Nor did Nina imagine or suspect her family were guilty of mail tampering and forgery with her handwriting.

Michael's Business Shop---Employed Lewis

Michael was employed in a factory that performed the same work he did in his own business: cut and mold fabric for men's hats. He refused to close his long-held business with men's hats and accessories. His shop was walking distance to and from home. His business made enough income to cover the shop's rent, utilities and other business expenses. Behind the retail section was a large room with a refrigerator, cooking range, sink, stand-up storage cabinet a table with two chairs, and a cot for napping. Also, a bathroom area with a flush toilet and a wash sink.

Lewis had no interest in the business of his parents after it was blacklisted without return to its past success. When sixteen years old, Lewis quit school for full time sales employment in a gift shop in the city's business section. He and his parents argued about room-and-board money from him. In a loud and firm voice, Lewis told them *it is the duty of parents to provide for their children until twenty-one years old. It means that none of my wages are given to parents for any reason.* His words were the same words already spoken by his Aunt Lucy and Linda.

Nina to Replace Lucy for Chester

Linda often called Lucy about duty to be Chester's bride. Lucy knew that gossip

about this duty marriage troubled her being pursued by the type man she wanted for a

husband. Lucy continued to believe that her good looks, nice shape, and prestige of her

family name allowed her to pick and choose who she married. The plan with her sister

Jean four years ago during Nina's continued care for burn injuries was now ready for use

to free Lucy of her duty marriage. When planned, it was without Michael's advance

knowledge or consent.

In new telephone talks with Linda, Lucy encouraged her to offer Jean part-time

waitress work to help her family's money needs. Michael permitted Jean to accept the

employment for five days weekly and the hours when their children were in school. Jean

was given the usual minimum hourly wage for waitresses with customer tips to increase

her take-home income.

Jean was on the job a few days when Lucy worked with Linda's history of

jealousy. "The children produced by Michael and my sister connect to the bloodline of

my birth family. This means my refusal to honor a duty marriage makes my fifteen-year-

old niece Nina *next in line* to be Chester's bride. It makes sense when duty to marry

Carlos was passed from the last in line of one family to first in line in the other family of cousins. With Nina as Chester's bride, duty to be Carlos' bride would pass to her younger sister Tricia as next and last in line to pay their family's debts. Chester wouldn't had to wait too long for a bride. Nina started womanhood two months ago. She turns sixteen years old in six months. She would then be two years older than the fourteen years minimum age this state allows for a girl to marry. With the right kind of work, it could happen with consent of her parents.

"But that's not everything. Nina would be a bride many years younger than Chester. He'd have a bride with good looks, nice shape, upper class qualities, and her school qualified high intelligence. All her qualities would make many jealous of Chester. It would give Chester and you bragging and boasting rights as happened for Michael after you gave him my sister Jean for marriage. With Nina as part of your wealthy family, a financially good life would repay your use of her with abandonment to punish the church who didn't honor your request for help."

"I owe nothing for what happened to the child. Everyone didn't have to share in what was planned. But I like your idea of Nina to replace you. Nothing made her interested in Carlos or in marriage. Work is needed to end Nina's goal of the convent after high school and to make her become interested in marriage. At twenty-seven-years of age, my son Chester shouldn't continue life much longer without a bride."

Linda's original rule was that a husband's ego would suffer, and he'd feel inferior if his wife was more educated or more intelligent than he. Linda changed her rules in favor of making people jealous of her and Chester---in favor of boasting and bragging rights. Linda didn't change her rules that marriages must produce children but now ignored medical predictions that Nina's life would be jeopardized if pregnant.

Linda followed Lucy's plan after making Jean her employee. Linda told Jean to take Nina to work with her on the coming Friday when a teacher's convention meant no student classes. While Jean worked in the diner, Linda's daughter Lynn and Nina were to spend four hours alone together in the apartment home above the diner. Twenty-year-old Lynn was four years older than Nina. Lynn used time together with talks about how good her two brothers always were to her:

"My brothers set up a party with a lot of guests and food to celebrate my graduation from high school last month. My brothers gave me this expensive wristwatch I'm wearing. The clothes I just took from the closet were more gifts from my brothers. One dress was for graduation day and the other dress for the graduation party. It's clear these are expensive clothes when a check is made of the fabric and tailoring work." During Lynn's talks about her brothers, she removed readymade sandwiches from the refrigerator for them to eat at the kitchen table. Lynn continued to talk about her brothers, the graduation party and her gifts as she polished her fingernails and toenails. Their visit ended four hours later with the end of Jean's workday.

While Nina and her father ate tan evening meal together, she told him about her time with Lynn that day. "I don't know why I was taken there nor why I was to spend time alone with her. She's part of family life and I never felt she was a real part of my life. I remember she was my sponsor for my Confirmation sacrament four years ago. That was the only time we connected with each other in eight years since my accident until today. She talked a lot, *a lot* about how good her brothers were with a celebration of her high school graduation. She said they arranged a big party for it with a lot of guests, food and their gifts to her that she wanted me to see. She said nothing about why our family wasn't invited to that big party and I didn't ask her why."

Michael's only response was, "I don't have an explanation for things now. Some things cannot be understood while it's happening."

After father and daughter finished their supper, Nina went to her bedroom where she continued to read a book. Michael said nothing to Jean about Nina's time with Lynn. He planned to first handle things with Linda when she visits, as he expected, after Sunday church services in two days.

———

Marriage Issues Revisited

Michael knew Linda would visit him today after mass ended. Aunt Lucy's presence in his home added to what he believed would be talk between him and Linda. He drank many cups of coffee while he sat on a chair at the kitchen table that faced his apartment door. The bell at the building's front door rang. Before the expected knock on the apartment door, Michael told Jean and their children, *Only I will open the door for whoever it is.*

Eleven-year-old Donald and nine-year-old Jerry were sent outdoors from the kitchen back door. Michael opened the apartment front door to see Linda---as he expected. While they walked to the kitchen, he told her, "I know what you're trying to do and it's not going to happen!"

Linda sat next to him to the kitchen table where Jean served them fresh cups of coffee. "Michael let us sit here to talk about things in calm and quiet ways. It's best that you send your girls out of the kitchen while we talk." Nina and Tricia sat on their bed only one room away from the kitchen where they could hear some of what their father and Linda talked about. Jean remained silent while Michael used his role as head of household for decisions concerning his family. Jean said nothing about her part in the plans for Nina to replace Lucy and Linda didn't say that Lucy introduced it.

Linda spoke with no wasted words. "Blood bonds include extended family. I arranged for you to have a prize for marriage. It's now your turn to repay me with a like gift! The younger one pays your debts. It would have been that way if nothing changed the older one's plan."

Michael replied, "Hope rests with only one. Nothing and no one could move the other one! It's been tried."

"No other choice is left for where duty lands. The rules were always clear that duty passed to the next younger one when older ones refused. Examples are close at hand for what happens to who refused to pay a debt." [The unspoken reference was the hurt life of Jean's sister Sarah who refused duty to marry Michael's brother Lance.]

Michael said, "You could lead a horse to water but cannot make it drink."

Linda's ruling voice said, "We talk about life, not about horses and water! My son has waited too many years for a bride. We have no answer for customers and neighbors who ask why he hasn't married yet. I don't want our family to be empty-handed for long years of spent money. Some people have called us fools for having spent so much money without any guaranty of the arranged returns. I don't want our family to feel like or be viewed as fools. *Do what must be done to make things happen and set a wedding date!*"

Michael took a deep breath and with an equally firm voice said, "*Think twice!!* You negotiated my debts. You would suffer as I would if those debts aren't paid. You know that our family group added people who punished divorce. Also, that who was punished for divorce has troubled the lives of who arranged it."

Tricia understood all she overheard while Nina's lost memory about family's ways prevented her from understanding it. Tricia and Nina went into the kitchen where Nina interrupted the adult talk: "We heard something about a wedding date. Who is it for? I know it couldn't be for me. I'm only fifteen years old with plans to enter the convent after high school graduation. And nuns are married to only God."

Linda's authoritative voice blurted, "The church has enough nuns to serve God and doesn't need to add you. You've had your years as a child. You bleed. You're now a woman. Women marry and deliver children."

"*I bleed?* I didn't fall, and there's no blood on my body. *I'm a woman!?!?* What are you talking about? I'm only fifteen years old and that is still only a girl. Family has always known my plan to be a nun. Maybe a nun nurse like the ones who cared for me in the hospital, like those who helped me to walk again, and those who cared for me in the outpatient clinic. They cared about me when my family proved to care nothing about me.

"I also don't understand why you say women must marry, or why someone *my age* must marry. Aunt Lucy is ten years older than I but still has no groom for a wedding day. Your daughter Lynn is four years older than I and also still without a groom and wedding day. Instead of Lynn married in her teen years, you allowed her to graduate high school. But you don't want me to have a high school education or become a nun. You change rules only when it suits you and benefits your family."

Linda said, "Lynn lost close bonds with her cousins Leslie and Paula when those girls took different life ways. Lynn stayed in high school to make friends. She needed girlfriends for when she goes to the movies, dances, shops for clothes and other things that girls do together."

Nina said, "Lynn still has her cousin Nancy and neither one wants college after high school. Lynn is five years older than Nancy; she could be an older sister for Nancy to help her through the loss of her older sisters."

"It's not possible outside of family life. Lynn has tried it. Lynn suffered embarrassment when seen with her in public where people stared at Nancy's image."

Nina continued: "Okay, let us put the subject back to marriage. What about a groom for Lynn from friends of her brothers?"

"That's another impossible thing. Both of her brothers have had no time to make friends. Their lives have been devoted to our diner business since they were fourteen years old. They work in the kitchen with their father and shop together for our business needs. Her brothers have been each other's friend throughout their lives. Other times, they were with people who are part of family for special occasions like weddings, christening of newborns, and special wedding anniversaries."

Aunt Lucy realized that talks strayed from making Nina Chester's bride--- wedding plans that would free her [Lucy] of duty to marry him.

Nina is Told Forgive and Forget

Aunt Lucy faced Nina. "You could not enter the convent without parental consent before you are twenty-one years old. You already know that won't happen and six years is a very long time from now to your twenty-first birthday."

"I'll ask someone in the church or in the convent about exceptions to that rule."

"If anyone from the church or convent helped you, they'd have to worry about legal charges for *aiding and abetting the delinquency of a minor*. That's no way to thank those who helped in all the ways you described. Above all else, you must learn all of what life holds and would be lost before your decision to enter the convent. The church always needs nuns. You could become a nun at any age."

"I could wait until legal age to enter the convent. I want to do something more than be a man's wife. Becoming a nun is not all that's available to grown women. I've read books about what and how some women contributed to the world. Examples are the lives of Mrs. Miniver and Florence Nightingale who didn't make marriage the only way of life."

Fourteen-year-old Tricia mumbled, "Aunt Lucy gave her those books."

Linda's loud ruling voice interrupted: "*Brides! Brides!* Our families cannot lose any more of our womenfolk. We don't need more educated and independent womenfolk. Leslie has her journalism degree and Paula is in college for a degree in something else. *Two brides lost that way are already too much.* Their loss lessens the size and growth of our families. We can't lose any more brides. Whoever strays from the fold for any reason must be punished."

Lucy interrupted and again faced Nina. "Books were written about those women because they were exceptions of the average women. In the real world, women live with parents until married because they rarely if ever earn enough wages to support themselves. Women aren't paid as much for their work even if it's the same work done by men. Marriage is a way of life for most women and not careers or as nuns in a convent."

Nina stood with her hands on the top of an empty chair at the kitchen table. "Books and observations of people let me know that marriage is not the always the best way of life. For years I've accepted why I could not and would not marry. I heard the hospital nun tell my mother that my scarred body would not make it possible to deliver children as our families expect with marriage. I remember when Linda said married men expect and want children. Family life makes it clear that marriage vows are commitments for the wives but allows husbands to stray without divorce. Family permits this while the Bible is not against divorce.

"Wives of this family are to forever stay with an abusive husband, a woman chasing husband, or a husband whose gambling and drinking habits fail to properly provide for his family. Abuse can be more than physical harm. It could be a husband who ignores his wife's feelings and needs and destroys her self-worth as a human so that only he matters. Maybe it's referred to as the husband's control to satisfy his ego. Such situations credit cousin Leslie for when she said women need an education for an ability to provide for selves with good and honest wage paying work, whether she does or doesn't marry. If I had an abusive husband or one who didn't do his duty to pay the bills, I'd leave him as the Bible allows---even after the wedding vows of *for better or worse.*

"Aside from all that, some families show pride when one of them chose to be a priest or nun---but not my family. I choose life as a nun no matter how my family feels about it. In the year I was hospitalized, I never heard any nun complain about her life. Nuns have the freedom to break vows, but none ever looked unhappy or talked about doing it."

Aunt Lucy responded, "Nuns are not a big percent of the world's population. Sex is an important part of marriage that produces the next generation for the world to continue. Sex is a natural part of life that sometimes results in unusual behavior between priests and nuns. Battles of husbands and wives are as normal as it is among children who grow up together. One example is the battle about who married who between your cousins Leslie, Paula and Nancy years ago. What other reason keeps you from wanting to marry?"

"I learned that nuns have a workday end that allows them to relax for meals and social time together. I compare that to my cousin Leslie's words that marriage in our families make servants and slaves of wives. There is also my observation that work never ends for our married women who must be wife, homemaker, and mother---with a greater workload if she must add wage paying work or help in her husband's business. Life is very different for husbands in our families. At the end of their workday and work week, they are free to do whatever wanted."

Aunt Lucy asked, "Why do you see marriage that way?"

"Recent examples come to mind: Our family were all at the table for a meal. My father asked me to leave where I sat on the other side of the table to get him a fork and spoon that was in a drawer behind him. Another example is that my brothers stay in bed until our mother takes their socks and underclothes from the night tables at their bedsides and hands them these things. It looks like my brothers are learning from young ages to see their wives as servants."

Michael said. "Those things don't make servants or slaves of womenfolk. It's normal and natural for women to care for their men folk. The school provides a little about homemaking, but girls learn most about it from their mother. What else makes you not want to marry?"

"If I see marriage as stressful for women, there must be some truth to what the nun told my mother. The nun said nerve damage and effects of multiple traumas made me unable to do what average girls and women do at any time in life. My inability to do all that a husband would expect could result in a lot of complaints or abuse from him that would hurt or destroy marriage. It sounds best that I keep marriage out of my life."

Michael told Nina, "Whether girls do or don't realize it, they copy much of what they see done by their mother as homemaker and family caretaker. You'd automatically find the strength to be like your mother to make marriage a good and safe place."

Nina gripped the chair tightly. Her voice trembled with attempts to hold back tears and anger as she said: "On top of all things, it seems that no one understands or cares about what I now put into words. I could never trust that a husband would give me unconditional love, loyalty and devotion. I could never believe a husband would be better than what I've experienced from my whole family!

"Laws, society, and growing children expect parents to care for, provide for, and protect them from harm. None of my family did any of it for me. Instead, church charity funds provided for all my needs. I was alone for near to a year in a bedridden condition with every desperate need, and helpless against abuse from children and their visitors in the room with me. When no adult was in our room, I slept with open eyes and ears to prevent the children from being at my bed during naps and nighttime sleep. Their visitors used my situation as an example of what happens to children who don't obey or misbehave. Patients in the room with me and their visitors refused to believe I only had an accident. They insisted I did something very bad to be punished with abandonment by all my big family.

"When patients were discharged from the hospital, the remaining patients and their visitors gossiped about my situation to the incoming patients and their visitors. My bedridden condition didn't give me a chance to get away from any of it. The hospital didn't have enough nurses to give me a private duty nurse to protect me from any of those things. Painful life continued when I was reclaimed. For almost two years of outpatient care, I was alone in a room far from my family in other parts of the apartment. My father gave different reasons why no family could be company for me. Those three years made me unable to trust or believe anyone."

Linda interrupted with her authoritative voice. "That's the past! You must forgive and forget. You've had a normal life since then."

"Nothing about my life into today has been normal. Your talk about forgive and forget doesn't fit this family. I've heard different adult family say someone *owed* them. I don't know who owes for what but know it means something from the past. It is some proof that this family does not forgive or forget. Yet I'm being asked to do what family does not do. This family has given me nothing when desperately needed and I owe it nothing. My lost three years has forever changed my life and made me forever different from my family---and different from most people of all ages. I had to forgive who made the mistake of returning me to family and had to learn how to accept it to go on with life after forced back to family. Return to family forced me to re-connect with them but hasn't made me feel a loving attachment."

Michael asked Nina, "Doesn't it mean something that we took you back into the fold?"

"No! Legal technicalities, new laws for families, and my young age allowed parents to reclaim me. When I was reclaimed, it was not an act of love but use of me for my parents to continue with public assistance. The *fold*, as you call it, includes my godparents [Linda and Paul] who haven't made me feel any concern for me. My godmother said *godparents have no duty while parents are alive and able to take wage paying work to provide for their family.*

"Before my release from the hospital, I heard Sister Rise tell my mother that all hospital clergy predicted nothing good with my return to family. What I've experienced since discharged from the hospital has made me agree with that prediction. In my two years as an out-patient, I saw a parent for the shortest amount of time. My father once spent enough time to tell me why no family had time for me. Once I was like normal, all adult family surrounded me, but none wanted to hear me talk about my lost years. No family wanted to look at my scarred and deformed body. Only my father looked at the scars below my swim wear when at the beach where he put cocoa butter on the skin graft scars to protect it from the sun."

Linda interrupted again with an authoritative voice. "What you experienced in life should have made you tough like the rest of your family! You had too many years with a governess who pampered, protected and taught high-class society ways to you, your sister and brothers. It's time for you five children to face life as it is for us."

"What I experienced kept me from wanting to be like the family I was born into. You want me to be tough, but nothing made your daughter [Lynn] tough. You don't allow Lynn to be in your business because you don't want her subjected to the bus and trolley drivers who are your customers. How you raise your children is your business but you're not my mother and not my father's mother. My father is head of our household, and I don't know why he has allowed you to have a say in our lives. The queen of England doesn't tell her people how to live life as a family. That's done by dictators such Germany's Hitler and Italy's Mussolini."

Linda's voice was again authoritatively loud. *"Enough talk! Nothing works! There's no value here to family life! Do what you must Michael for the needs and growth of The Family."*

As Linda readied herself to depart, she said to whoever listened, "It's clear that a search must be made to give my daughter a groom. The wealth of our family qualifies for the book of *Who's Who* as one way to get a groom."

Tricia said, "You won't know if he'd have equally wealthy parents or his own wealth. He could be an opportunist looking for an easy way to better his life."

Linda said, "We'd know or learn the difference before a wedding day is fixed. Michael, I look forward to good news very soon. If not, you know what must be done."

Michael replied, "But ignorance and pure innocence exist!"

"When years of our tax papers were audited, my husband and I were told that innocence and ignorance of the law was no excuse. We had to repay the Internal Revenue a large sum of money with interest and penalty charges for that mistake. Family rules also do not forgive ignorance or innocence. Now call for a taxi to get me home."

All Are Mad at Someone

Two weeks passed since the unsuccessful talk to replace Lucy with Nina as the bride for Chester. Linda continued to telephone Lucy about duty to be Chester's bride. Lucy encouraged Linda to make another attempt for Nina to replace her, and knew Linda would do it with another visit to Michael after Sunday church services. Before Linda's expected arrival, Lucy was in Michael's living room with Nina, Tricia and the Sunday newspapers.

Linda took the bus from the church to Michael's home. When he opened the apartment door, he was surprised to see Linda. She followed him to the kitchen table where they faced each other. Jean again remained quiet, served them coffee and refilled their cups.

Linda put her cup down. "I've come for you to tell me what's been done. We have a woman and not a child. Do I get returns for years of spent money? Do I get the returned favor of a prize for my son?"

"It's the same situation. One could not be worked in any direction. The other could not be pushed further. The debts remain with my family but are equally your debts as the one who pursued use of the church and the legal advice to reclaim."

"You didn't have to use the favors that benefited your family---but you did. I'm here for your final word about a bride for my son. Your refusal to give consent makes the other one equally guilty of the refusal. I remind you what happens when things aren't made right. *To the dogs! Eat words and ways however it most hurts!*"

Nina went to the kitchen and interrupted their talk to ask her father. "What did Aunt Linda mean when she said *to the dogs?* She has no dogs and we have no dogs. The way people talked when I was in the hospital became normal. The talk between the two of you and from other family doesn't sound like other people."

Michael said, "Your godmother sometimes wants to offer her customers a new recipe or make changes in a used recipe's flavor and texture. If the finished recipe doesn't taste right to her, the food is still good but given to stray dogs instead of to her customers."

"What does she mean when she said *eat words and ways?* Who does that and how?"

"You misunderstood your godmother's words. What she said was 'curds and whey'. It's part of a child's nursery rhyme that goes like this, *Little Miss Muffet sat on a buffet, eating her curds and whey when along …...*"

Linda interrupted and told Michael to call a taxi to get her home. Nina re-joined Tricia and Aunt Lucy in the living room with Jean behind her. The taxi was in front of the building when Linda left for it without anything more said that day between her and Michael.

Lucy went to the kitchen to where Michael was seated at the table. She looked straight at him, and with a sarcastic tone of voice said, *"You can't do it to your own!!!"*

Michael didn't respond but understood Lucy would join the punishment for Nina's refusal to marry and not replace Lucy as Chester's bride. Michael know that Nina would be given to people that would include boys rejected by everyone before her and now unable to take another rejection.

Nina heard her father's mumbled words as he left Lucy and walked to the kitchen back door: "The impossible is expected for one person to be and do all things. Everyone put their eggs in one basket." After that, he told everyone, "I'm going outdoors for a long walk alone to think!"

After Michael left, Lucy smiled with her words to Jean: *"Looks like your two girls are in the same situation as your sisters. Love me, love my children; hate me, hate my children."* Jean silently recalled the meeting with her sisters five years earlier when they said, "We wonder how you'd feel if your daughters suffered as your sisters have suffered since you married!"

During Michael's walk alone, he thought about the wants of different family who want to use Nina for their troubled lives. He realized that Nina had no fighting chance for a win against them no matter what decision he made for her. The group of families had their own connections to hurt and even destroy Nina's life beyond repair if she wasn't made to service them. He also recalled Linda's copies of the tax audits that showed how many years and how much money provided for the siblings and parents of his wife. This provided Linda with the power to use his wife's birth family and extended family however wanted. Michael also knew that his wife's birth and extended family didn't want to lose the honor, prestige and benefits with their family name on maps of Italy. Michael thought of who and why different family would be part of Nina's arranged punishment:

---Nina survival after abandoned is a permanent sore for all family to suffer scorn and shame since reclaimed.

---Nina's parents had no cashed checks to the hospital or receipts from it that show payment of her medical care.

---Jealousies worsened when school tests proved Nina had the IQ of a twenty-year-old instead of her then eleven years.

--- Linda, Bertha and Julie's husband Lance wanted him [Michael] punished for boasts about his wife and children.

Linda wanted Michael punished for his inability or unwillingness to make Nina become Chester's bride.

---Linda's family group felt used and viewed as fools without returns of marriage mates for years of spent money.

---Julie and her siblings would feel used and made to be fools if marriages for children of the divorced weren't kept.

--- Lance would lose face if the duty marriages he arranged for children of his wife's divorced brother wasn't kept.

--- Julie and her priest brothers would feel cheated if tricks didn't make Nina become Carlos' bride after their work for the hospital to save her life.

---Lawyer Benji would feel cheated if tricks didn't make Nina become Carlos' bride after his free legal advice for Nina to be reclaimed without charges against her parents.

--- If Nina wasn't made to marry Carlos, Linda would be punished for having obtained the help of the priests and the lawyer to benefit Michael's family.

---Lewis needed Nina to marry Carlos for belief of the lies that it would free him of punishment for refusal to marry Carlos' sister.

---Carlos would again chase Lewis for making him believe Nina would be his bride as returns for protection of her in earlier years---and making Carlos feel that he was made a fool.

---If Nina didn't become Carlos' bride, he and mother would view it as more punishment for divorce. This would make them return to troubling lives of Julie's siblings, and lawyer Benji's career into his family.

---Tricia would join the arranged punishments of Nina if duty to marry Carlos passed to her as last in line.

---Tricia would blame Lewis for passing duty to marry Carlos to his sisters. She would join the punishment for his refusal to marry Carlos' sister.

Michael suspected that Lucy would work in two connected doctors to join the arranged punishments of Nina.

Michael knew it was a life in which nothing was for free, not even friendship. He knew that Lucy had much help for Nina's punishment and understood the process: End Nina's plan to be a nun and put her into the dating world. End Nina's plan for continued education. Mold Nina to speak without thinking for the activities to make her *eat words and ways*.

When Michael returned home, he joined Lucy at the kitchen table. Jean quickly served them a cup of coffee. Lucy opened punishment work: "Nina let's start a *new game.* Answer what your father and I say with the first words that come to your mind. It must be quick responses. You must not pause to think about if your answer sounds right or wrong, good or bad."

"Why is this game for only me? Why doesn't it include my sister and brothers?"

Aunt Lucy said, "Your sister and brothers know this game and are socially active while you spend most of your time alone to read books. You need to learn how other people make conversation before old enough to enter the convent. People ask questions to know a person. Quick responses are proof that you told the truth and didn't think about what would sound good or the best way to say it. You must show that you have personal likes and dislikes about people, things and activities---show an active mind and express your opinions about everyone and all things. Your father and I will do this until we feel convinced that you have this needed habit for social conversations."

Michael and Nina were later alone together in one of their walks outdoor. His silent guilt needed a way to guide Nina's responses in the social life she was to be pushed into. He told her, "Never say anything bad about anyone. Always remember this expression, *there but for you go I.* It's another form of the Bible's words that says *do unto others as you would want done to you.*"

All who know you have known that you hold forgiving ways expected of the nun you plan to become. All who know you also know you wouldn't think or say bad, but I felt that a reminder of the Bible's words couldn't hurt."

Linda's Spite-work

Although Linda ruled her marriage, she knew that Jean honored Michael as head of household to make all decisions for their family. Jean remained an employee of Linda and Paul. At no time did Linda tell Jean she forgave Michael's refusal to give Nina to Chester. Linda knew she could work things that would hurt Michael's family in more than one way: Jean would not be home for when their children were not in school weekdays and vacation periods---not be home early to have meals ready for scheduled mealtime---and not continue as her employee.

First, Linda lengthened Jean's daily work hours. In the longer hours, Jean was to refill containers with sugar, salt, pepper, ketchup, mustard, mayonnaise, and napkin holders. Before now, Linda did not realize this allowed Jean to notice that she took leftover food of customers to the kitchen instead of to garbage containers fixed between the customer area and kitchen. No customers were there then when Jean saw this. Paul was relaxed in the customer area with a cup of coffee, shoes off and feet on a chair.

In a relaxed family way, Jean informed Paul and Linda that re-serving leftover food of customers was against the law. Linda accepted Paul's decision to end the practice from then onward. However, Linda was silently concerned that Jean might report this past practice to the authorities. Linda feared the possibility of a large financial penalty as done with tax returns. She feared the possibilities that their successful business operations could be shut down, gossip that would worry customers if not shut down, and lost prestige as business owners if forced to close business operations.

Linda extended Jean's workdays and hours to include Saturdays. This dramatically decreased Jean home and family time as homemaker and mother of teenaged children as well as work to finish hats that Michael molded. Jean voluntarily quit. This freed Linda of blame that she didn't care about the family's money needs of Michael's family, but it didn't free her of worry about food handling and food serving laws.

Linda knew people with a bad reputation weren't always believed or trusted. Every table was filled with customers when some of them asked about Jean's absence. Linda said Jean was discharged because she was overly friendly in flirtatious ways with bus drivers and didn't want that reputation for her business. Linda didn't respond when bus drivers told her that Jean gave them only very good service with a good disposition and little talk while she took their food orders and served it to them.

* * * * * * * * * * * * * *

Linda wasn't satisfied with only her spite work for Jean to voluntarily quit. She also wanted Michael to lose Jean---the prize she arranged for him to marry twenty-one years ago.

Linda knew that Lucy would also service this at the same time it would service herself with a duty marriage she refused.

Lewis Rejects Father's Advice

Lewis didn't like military life and didn't like the lost time to do something with

his life. Doctor Robert's report that Lewis had a heart murmur helped him to be

discharged from navy boot camp. The report about a heart murmur was not untrue; it was

a part of Lewis' growing many inches taller in a short time. Lewis was back in civilian

life when Michael made another attempt for him to take duty to marry Carlos' sister.

Father and son battled this and other issues in Lewis' bedroom:

"Lewis, we can't undo what's been done. Examples of how much worse life could

be are with your mother's family. We must deal with how things are now. Be charitable.

Think of others. Be a friend and a companion for the boy [Carlos]. Take the place of his

run-away brother and share the parent duty. Teach mother and son civilized life. Help

him to do something with life. Whichever of your sisters takes the duty to marry him

would be crushed without you in it for her protection. Don't be ruled by selfishness and

greed! Don't be bought or involved with money passing! Once in this life, there's no

getting out until people behind things decide when and how it ends for you. Rewards

aren't worth what it does to your life and to the lives of your loved ones. It's been my life

but it doesn't have to be your life unless *you* make it. I know what I speak about."

Lewis emphasized his responses with fisted punches into a metal clothes closet in his bedroom. "I have nothing in common with that boy! Charity begins at home and my life is my home! I'm an American and don't want your Old Country ways. No one had the right to speak on my behalf or to arrange my future without my permission. I want to marry someone I could be proud to be seen with and who could give me beautiful children. I don't want the possibility of producing children to suffer because their looks and shapes are different from most people.

"I lost friendships and much time from school because that boy chased after me. He was at me before the bell to begin the school day and during lunch breaks. When I didn't go to my classes for roll call, classmates responded for me to be marked present; my friends gave me the assigned homework to graduate grade school as scheduled. After I used what was offered [Nina] to get that boy's interest away from me, I was able to be back in school for every class. As for my help to teach them civilized life, people don't like it when anyone tries to change them. It makes them feel put down and starts resentment that grows. People who want to change life pay attention to people with the ways they want and copy it to make their own changes. You can't put brains where there are none. He learned to read and write before he was discharged from the navy but has done nothing to better his life. He was in the navy long enough to qualify for all veteran benefits. With discharge, he was told about government help to veterans to further their education or learn job skills with a shorter time into good wage paying work, but he hasn't used any of it. He's two and one-half years older than I am and shows no sign of doing anything to better his life.

"I don't want to be held back in life by anything or anyone! The accident kept me from parents who could afford my having the best education to do something with life.

People have a limited number of years to do something with life. I don't want to end up poor and alone in a home for old poor people like my mother's father. I wasn't in military service long enough to qualify for any veteran benefits. All I want must be my work. I want a one family house with a two-car garage in a good area for my wife and our children. I want big enough savings to enjoy life's Golden Years. I want to be someone people look up to, respect and admire for all achieved.

"I learned how to keep people busy with other people and other things to keep trouble away from my doors. I have a lot of lost time to make up. For the past eight years I haven't had the good that other boys have had from their parents like cars and spending money. I quit school when sixteen years old to have my own money. I want time with boys who aren't of nearby families or part of our families. I treat dates very good; I'm not labeled cheap. I have a right to keep all my earnings before and after discharged from the navy. It's the parents' duty to provide for their children until twenty-one years old, and my twenty-first birthday is three years away.

"I don't care which of my sisters takes the duty to marry that boy, nor do I care what it does to either sister. They must learn how to protect and stand up for themselves like girls without brothers---as done by our cousins Leslie, Paula and Nancy."

Michel interrupted Lewis' rampage. "Those cousins had an advantage that your sisters haven't had. The growing years of those cousins put them with people of all type and kind in the tavern business of their parents; it helped them learn how to take care of themselves in a variety of situations. You know that our earlier years with a governess protected your sisters and taught them to be refined growing girls. Your sisters were always different from those cousins and cannot be compared to them. Don't join the gang that picks one person to suffer alone. United we stand as a family; divided we all fall one by one."

"My sisters are now teenagers! If they refuse to marry who is arranged, they must learn to protect themselves in the dating world."

"Listen to me. People behind things keep records of what a person does, says, and writes; it includes people who service things. The records are used to make a person *eat words and ways* and includes who is no longer needed. This work pulls in and uses loved and innocent children to punish their parents for whatever reason. The work sometimes uses an unsuspected person. All is done while people behind things hold clean hands. It produces what the Bible says about things passing from one generation to the next generation. Don't ruin your life and the lives of children you may produce. Don't make a circus of our family."

Lewis' voice was loudly strong: "I know how to live in this dog-eat-dog life. I know how to play dumb like a fox. I like wheeling and dealing with money. I like money. My parents made a circus of our family, not me! Nothing I do changes what parents did to this family."

Michael took a deep breath and calmly said, "Don't make things worse. People you step on to climb ladders await your fall down the ladders. I've done my fatherly duty to protect flesh and blood. I now have a clean conscience however and wherever the chips may fall for you." While Lewis walked away without another word, Michael said, "There's none so deaf as those who could hear but ignore and reject good advice."

Lucy and the Church

Lucy went to the church rectory for a priest's help about her duty marriage. After the church, Lucy went to Jean's home where she [Lucy] vented her anger. She removed all religious items in Jean's home and put them in the garbage as she said, "Even the church makes money its God! The church gives only lip service, talks about free will, dirty houses, and money to the church, *but not the help asked for*! There'll be a Hell on Earth that not even Jesus Christ can do anything about! Everyone eats their words and ways however it most hurts life and however long it takes to make it happen! All pay in one way or another at some time in life! Innocence and ignorance are not excused! Can't help who must get hurt and who must suffer along the way! The writing is on the wall! Everyone does what's best for self!"

Tricia told Nina, "Dad started everything."

Aunt Lucy interrupted Tricia to tell Nina, "Don't listen to or believe all from your sister. She has a convenient memory. She doesn't always know the true or full cause of history and doesn't always speak accurate conclusions!"

Lucy returned to venting her anger: "Vows of poverty from priests and nuns is separate from their church who needs and wants money as much as other people. Vatican City is very elaborate and costly to maintain. Catholic churches are expensive to own, maintain and repair. It has glass stained windows, murals, statutes, land that the church sits on and all that surrounds its structure. Clothes worn by the pope, cardinals, bishops, and other servants of God are more expensive than what most working people could afford for selves. The wages of most people also cannot afford the expensive cars used by cloth wearing church people.

"Priests and nuns say they do God's work but prove no different from other people who want promotions and to be top dog. Priests and nuns live unnatural lives while other people know that sex is a normal part of life and necessary to create the next generation. Priests and nuns will someday wear clothes that won't separate them from people in the world outside of the church. They'll someday need to share parent duty instead of escaping it by wearing the cloth. They'll someday be subjected to all the temptations and risks that happen to other people. Someday priests and nuns would prove to not protect their own and leave whoever is troubled to stand alone with whatever trouble or problem. The church will someday experience needs to clean a dirty house. It would learn to accept divorce like the Bible permits. The church has hypocrites on both sides. Many people attend church services as a social status. Some people make church a fashion show where they wear fine clothes and look to see how the other people in church are dressed. *Blood money*! Do and say what's needed for the public. What's said and done behind closed doors is word for word."

Lucy's monologue differed from the few words matriarch Linda used for the hospital nuns and priests seven years earlier when Nina was reclaimed: "Judge and be judged! Condemn and be condemned!"

[Decades later, the Catholic Church and its cloth wearing servants suffered all that

Lucy and Linda predicted.]

The next day was Sunday, Lucy was with her parents when they visited Jean and the first

grandchildren for Donald and wife Patricia. Lucy blamed her father as the first of different family whom she said was responsible for her hurt life. She now aimed to hurt his relationship with these grandchildren when she told them: "The cigar smell on his breath would make you sick to the stomach if you kissed him. The smell of wine on his breath is like being in an old men's saloon. His cigar smoke fills the home and makes clothes stink of smoke as it would do to your clothes if you hugged him."

The next day, Lucy visited Jean where she complained about her duty to care for their parents. Lucy demanded a meeting of brothers and sisters to discuss matters about their parents.

Sarah traveled from the next state for the meeting in Jean's home. Rocco and Caesar attended the meeting without their wives. Michael knew he had no say about anything they discussed and went to his business shop. Their four young children were sent outdoor for his wife and her siblings to privately discuss matters.

The five adult siblings were seated at the kitchen table when Lucy announced, "I won't support a father who put money ahead of his children's happiness. *A father who sold his children!"* The meeting ended with all in agreement to separate parents. All agreed that Lucy, as the last unmarried one home, would remain with their mother. All agreed they could not move forward until parents become American citizens. At a family gathering with parents in Jean's home, siblings took turns to encourage parents for it with similar words: "All your children are American citizens with birth here. It's time that you two become American citizens after thirty-five years in this country."

After parents became American citizens, application was made to place Donald in a home for the aging poor people. Before placement, the agency processed the required check of each adult offspring for the ability or inability to physically care for and/or financially contribute to the costs of his placement. The agency's decision freed them all of everything.

When Jean's children asked about this grandfather, Lucy said, "He's in a place that doesn't allow children." After Lucy said this, she mumbled, "*He'll die of a broken heart with throw-away punishment.*" No comment or questions were made about this.

Donald died without a church Mass or procession as practiced by their ethnic group and their church. Lucy discouraged Jean and Jean's children from wearing black clothes and black arm bands to honor the now deceased. After Donald's placement, his first son Rocco became head of the family: his four siblings and mother, his blood connected nieces and nephews.

Michael knew he had no say about the parent issues of his wife and her siblings. However, he felt the right to say something about them if he believed it would affect their lives and lives of their five children. Michael's observations of Sarah and Lucy with their children caused him to warn Jean that her sisters were working to hurt their lives. He urged Jean to break bonds with her siblings or to keep them at a distance. Jean refused to think or suspect that the brothers and sisters she helped to raise would arrange anything to deliberately hurt her life or the lives of her growing children.

Lucy's Services for Linda

Lucy's forward moving work included service for Linda. A part of this work for Linda included what Lucy wanted for different reasons. Lucy doesn't forget that Linda holds copies of tax return audits that listed her [Lucy] as a dependent for eleven years.

Lucy was often in Jean's home without their mother who was supposedly napping or sewing. On a Sunday that Lucy was in Jean's home, and when Michael left to find their two youngest sons for the family meal, Lucy spoke to Nina in a hurried way: "Take sides. Family situations are bigger than the famous feuds of the Hatfields and McCoys".

"Take sides for what? I can't take sides with any family part. All family is guilty of what was done to me. I'll stay neutral like Switzerland is for the world. I won't be part of family feuds when I'm a nun and it would help me to be and stay in the neutral zone."

Michael returned with his sons and before they were at the kitchen table, Lucy was again heard mumbling: "Misery wants company. Misery gets company." Lucy thereafter began another subject before Nina could ask for an explanation of the muttered words. At the table, Lucy asked Tricia, "Do you know what type person you want to marry when you're old enough?"

Fourteen-year-old Tricia quickly and firmly said, "I certainly do! And I could be choosy about a husband because my body has no scars and is not deformed. Boys want girls who have good looks and nice shapes. They're attracted to this before they know if a girl does or doesn't have smart brains. And most boys don't want their ego hurt with girls who are smarter than they are. I don't want to marry anyone who has the looks and life ways of my father's family. And I don't want to marry any grease-ball. Whom I marry would have good looks like I do. He'd be about five feet ten inches tall, not fat or skinny, but right for his height and bone structure. He'd have a college degree or some college. His looks and ways would be refined with civilized ways. He'd wear business suits to work. He'd provide well or have rich parents to help until success of his career work. He'd like the fine things in life for the family we'd make. We'd live in the best areas where our children would be in the best schools, and we'd all have good quality friends."

Aunt Lucy said, "What you want for marriage is like what I want. You and I have like situations of probable punishments if not freed of our duty." Lucy's words created another bond between her and Tricia for uses of this niece.

Lucy asked Lewis, "What about your future? What type do you want for a bride? What kind of marriage do you want for you and her?"

"I also know what I want, and it's not people like my father's family! I want a chance for children whose good looks and nice shape won't make them suffer when compared to others. My dirty blonde color hair and blue eyes lets me aim for the Polish speaking people who have good looks, blonde hair and blue eyes. I already have records to learn the Polish language, its music and its dances."

A Bride for Lewis

After leftover food was put away, Jean washed dishes, silverware, and cookware. Nina and Tricia dried it all and stored it for next use. Except Michael, all left the apartment to walk in the outside fresh air. Michael rested quietly to think about his family and family life. He felt trapped in a difficult and irreversible situation: If either daughter became Carlos' bride, she'd be destroyed by him and his mother without the protection of their brother Lewis married to Carlos' sister. Michael now telephoned Linda to report all that happened today.

"Don't worry Michael. Bertha and I would find ways to deal with things about Lewis. My diner brings adult customers of different ethnicity with different wants and needs. It's the same or greater for customers to the tavern of Bertha and Wayne where some people take their children of all ages for family meals. Tavern customers include people who use the juke box music with a free dance area and a pool table in another free area. Lewis likes all the tavern activity and attention to him as a nephew of its owners. He is never out of place in the tavern because of the family atmosphere, visits to his Uncle Wayne, Aunt Bertha and their daughters who are his cousins, Leslie, Paula and Nancy. His cousins help in the tavern and take time from duties to eat meals there. They have many chances to make friends of all type and kind. Nancy is the most socially active in the tavern where she sits at tables that have girls in her age range."

Alexis and her Polish speaking family were in the tavern when seventeen-year-old Lewis and she met each other. He was immediately attracted to her as she walked from the tavern dance floor to a table where people were seated. She had blonde hair, blue eyes, nice shape, and tall enough for Lewis' six-foot height. She resembled a famous beautiful singer-actress. Nancy took Lewis to where Alexis sat with her siblings and parents where she introduced Lewis to them. Alexis and her parents lived walking distance to and from the tavern; Lewis walked past their home on his way to and from the tavern. He loved the attention given to him when seen anywhere with Alexis.

For the coming twentieth wedding anniversary party of Alexis' parents, this tavern was chosen. Lewis was given permission to take his teenaged sisters with him to this celebration. Aunt Lucy and Tricia fixed Nina in every attractive way for attention: Tricia put Nina's black wavy hair in an upsweep with waves and curls around her face. Aunt Lucy applied Nina's face make-up to accentuate her hazel green eyes. Aunt Lucy also chose the clothes for Nina to wear that would show Nina's petite full figure.

Aunt Lucy's private talk with Tricia instructed her to keep a low profile and to encourage Nina to befriend a boy that appealed to her [Tricia]. Tricia would thereafter ask Nina what she learned about him. If the boy didn't meet Tricia's specifications, gossip would interpret Nina's time with him for his belief that she is interested in him. Tricia would not suffer any gossip or faulting in connection with that boy.

In a separate part of the tavern, Leslie, Paula and Nancy set up a group of long tables with chairs, chinaware, silverware, napkins, glasses and cups. As guests arrived, the girls put bowls and platters of food on a counter for guests to serve themselves.

Under-aged guests were served non-alcoholic beverages while alcoholic drinks were served to adults of legal drinking age. Aunt Lucy's instructions for Tricia weren't used when Tricia saw no boy here that appealed to her.

Lewis and Alexis steadily dated only each other for several weeks before he was drafted for military duty. When Lewis was ready to leave for navy boot camp, he told his family that he and Alexis were no longer together. He offered no explanation for their breakup nor talked about her after its end. After Doctor Robert helped Lewis' discharge from the navy while in boot camp, the tavern was the first place Lewis visited. It was when families with growing children had meals there, and others were there for the juke box music, the pool tables, and alcoholic drinks. Lewis had just entered the tavern when he heard his cousin Nancy's voice. They waved to each other and met a short distance away from the table that Nancy left.

After a brief chat with each other, Nancy walked Lewis about the tavern and introduced him to new groups of customers. The last introduction was with the family she left to greet him. It was a widowed mother with three grown children: Olive who remained seated next to her mother and her brothers Nick and Steve who stood up to shake hands with Lewis and an invitation for him to join them. Nany remained at this table.

"Thank you for the offer but I want to roam about to see if there is anyone I know from earlier times." Lewis didn't ask Nancy about Alexis. He wanted to see if Alexis was in the tavern, and if she had a new man in her life. Alexis was not there. Lewis found people who were their mutual friends and said Alexis had a new man in her life with wedding plans. Lewis left the tavern after he said *goodnight* to his family, people he knew, and people introduced to that night.

Olive and her family had what Lewis wanted for marriage: blonde hair, blue eyes and fair complexion. Nancy and Olive became friends before Lewis revisited the tavern. Nineteen-year-old Olive and seventeen-year-old Nancy felt bonded when they told each other about their traumatic experiences in grade school. Both continued to worry about if they'd ever be married.

"Nancy, I could never forget what I suffered from two brothers when in grade school. In the school playground before the start of a school day and during lunch break, they laughed loudly while they humiliated, embarrassed, harassed and ridiculed me because of my weight. They said I was like a hippopotamus who had to turn sideways to get through doors. Their body motions were to mimic what it was supposed to look like. They repeated those things for every day of school with all students waiting for the bell to ring for classes. Everyone always heard all they said and did about me. I'll never be able to forget that time in life for as long as I live.

"The school system could do nothing because the brothers never touched me or did anything to physically hurt me. My two brothers talked like big brothers to those younger brothers, Peter and Ernie but it changed nothing. My brothers learned that their co-worker Eric was the father of Peter and Ernie. Eric had seniority and job security in the workplace. When my brothers told Eric about the situation, he only told them *boys will be boys*---no apology and no interest to correct the behavior of his sons. In the workplace a few weeks later, Eric said his son Peter suffered a traumatic experience that caused him to have an uncontrollable severe stuttering condition. Eric didn't accuse my brothers of being responsible for it, but their working conditions became very stressful. It has been an uncomfortably tricky situation for my brothers, but they won't quit their jobs."

"Olive, at least you're no longer in that school or in that city part. I understand permanent emotional scars, but I've learned to live with my never-ending pain. As is obvious, I was born with very large bone structure that shaped me in different ways from most people. Many people and children at school labeled me a *monkey in a human body*. Though my family doesn't use that label with me, I'm always reminded of my unusual difference when I look in the mirror. My pain increases when with my cousins Nina md Tricia who have good looks and nice shapes. If I am lucky enough to marry, it could make me feel accepted as a human. Meanwhile, I live with the pain of my looks and shape. Let's talk about other things."

"We could change the subject to your cousin Lewis. I like his looks and baby face that hides his age. It would make many people jealous of me if we were seen together. Jealousy would grow if we married each other and he provided well so I wouldn't have to help with employment away from home. Especially since I don't like having to punch and employer's time clock. Jealousy would increase if he provided a home with a lot of space for my gardening hobby and if he planned a good life for the Golden Years."

"Olive, I can't change the size and shape of my body but it's different for you. You could lose weight and become desirable to Lewis."

"How? Doctors have said I'm more than overweight. Obese is what they said."

"It's important to know that Lewis chose to pick his bride from Polish speaking families. He has records at home to learn the Polish language, its music and dances. Your first step is to lose a lot of weight When that's done, you'd be ready for a new and final wardrobe."

"It would take a very long time for me to lose enough weight for just an average size figure. A doctor explained the weight loss process. And more than one clothing size would be needed during weight loss. After a big weight loss, surgery would be needed to remove excess skin. The project requires a lot of money and a long time from start to end. My brothers now help our family money needs. It ends when they marry and then falls on me to help her as the last unmarried one home. And we can't ignore that Lewis could meet someone to marry before I'm ready to be put into his life."

"I must check with my family about things. I'll get back to you with answers in a few days. Meanwhile, think positively."

After Nancy told her family about Olive and her interest in Lewis, Linda said, "It sounds like Olive is not yet employed and has much free time. Tell her that your family would help in every way for the future she wants. We'd provide and pay costs of a qualified person for her to lose weight. We'd pay the costs of new clothing sizes with weight loss along the way. We'd pay for a qualified doctor to surgically remove the excess skin after weight loss and pay for her final new wardrobe. Let her know she could expect Lewis as her groom and that he would provide well. Tell her that our returns would be for her to do whatever we'd want or need. Also, that it would require her to work with, for, or against Lewis and different parts of his family."

"Could I tell Olive some of what she might be asked to do?"

Linda firmly said, "No! We would give her instructions when and as needed after she becomes part of our families. Our part now is to help her get what she wants which is to lose weight, a new wardrobe, have Lewis for her groom, and have him provide well into life's Golden Years. But she must be told some things in advance that includes Lewis is to be punished for refusal of a duty marriage. Also tell her about his dark side which is that he pushed you down a long flight of steps, laughed as you fell and laughed as you climbed back up the steps. Also tell her that Lewis punched his sister Nina in her face so hard that it caused heavy nose bleeding and a broken nose bone. If Olive could accept all these things about him and still wants Lewis for her groom, a successful outcome puts her in debt to us until we free her.

"There is more you should tell Olive before she joins us. When she is married to Lewis, she must know beforehand that her birth family and its connections would become part of our families. When her family is part of us, we would help to free her brothers of discomfort in their workplace. When this time comes, we'd need Olive's brothers to get recent pictures of their supervisor's stuttering son and information about the boy's ongoing life. Things could make one of Michael's daughters be that boy's bride. Olive should know that Lewis' Aunt Lucy would oversee things for the activities while doing her own share of the work. It means that Olive must have a good relationship with his Aunt Lucy."

* * * * * * * * * * * * * * * * * *

During the process of Olive's changed life, Uncle Lance taught her how to imitate handwritings to be used for whatever reason or purpose. She was told in advance that it was forgery and a punishable crime if proven. She was also told that Uncle Lance committed forgery very many times and was never accused of or punished for the crime."

Tricia, Nancy and [Nancy's] mother heard Olive say, "I'd trust being safe among your families. I'm willing to do anything for money."

Olive's first job with forgery connected with Nancy's sister Leslie who departed family roots with a journalism degree and promised to later help Nina to also leave family roots.

Felix and Allen were brothers. Their father, Sam was a co-worker of Donald who sold his growing children to be future marriage mates for children of Linda and for Lance. Donald helped Sam to receive financial help from Linda and Lance to open a barber shop with employees.

Felix and Allen operated a butcher shop with groceries. Jean and Lucy shopped there together and separately. Felix, Allen and their siblings were close in age to Donald's children Jean, Sarah, Lucy, Rocco and Caesar who referred to each other as cousins. Felix was discharged from the army with lifetime disability income. Allen suffered traumatically in military combat but it did not qualify for lifetime disability. Bachelor Allen was younger than married Felix. To not hurt Felix' disability income, Allen was the registered owner and Felix a silent partner of this business. This gave Allen the upper hands in business operations. Lucy knew this arrangement and used it to her advantage whenever and however wanted.

Felix and Allen equally shared in business profits since they worked in it for the same number of days and hours. Their different ways with this business were pronounced with the government's food stamp program: Allen didn't always collect the food coupons, but Felix always followed the rules of this program. Their business partnership ended when Felix refused continued risks of disability income, and its end caused Felix to hold a grudge against Allen. Felix looked forward to when life would also make Allen a financial loser---no matter how long it took to happen.

Linda would not forget or forgive Allen's rejection of her daughter Lynn for marriage in the earlier years. Lucy was to service Linda's want for him to suffer rejection. Felix and Allen did not yet break their business partnership when Lucy showed them recent pictures of Nina. Days later, Lucy told Jean, "Nina is fifteen and one-half years old. It's time for her to learn how to shop for foodstuff. It could start with the butter you need. You could let her get it from where you usually buy it, the shop that our cousins Felix and Allen own. Their store is on the corner less than one block from here."

Jean didn't have a food coupon for butter when Nina was sent for it on Saturday. When Nina entered the shop, Felix was cutting meat for counter display while Allen served the morning customers. Nina waited for Allen to ask, "What can I get for you?" but it didn't happen until all the other customers were served and left the shop. When Allen gave Nina the butter, he didn't ask her for the required food coupon as she heard him do with all customers before her.

Nina was gone longer than expected for an item that didn't need to be weighed or cut. When back home, Jean quickly pushed her to the kitchen's corner wall. Jean's angry eyes were fixed on Nina's injured stomach where her fists repeatedly punched. Tricia and Aunt Lucy stayed seated at the kitchen table where they watched the beating. When Jean stopped, Nina asked her, "What was the beating for?" As Jean continued to not answer, Tricia volunteered, "It was because of a lie I told." When Tricia said this, Jean's eyes suddenly had a blank look while in front of Nina; Jean then walked away from Nina to the sink for a glass of water.

Nina went to her sister with questions. "Why did you lie about me? What did you lie about? What made your lie believable?" Tricia kept a wide smile on her face as Nina walked closer to her. Tricia's refusals to answer the questions made Nina behave against her natural ways. She struck Tricia on a shoulder with an open hand. Aunt Lucy interfered after one strike:

"In genteel and refined society such as the family your mother and I were born into, well-bred women don't physically attack each other. They discuss matters with each other. Well-bred women also don't give people anything to gossip about. It's best for both of you to forget what just happened and forget the past for new starts as sisters. You need to end gossip about the bad blood between you two. New friends that either of you make would not want to be part of the trouble between sisters."

Near to when Allen and Felix closed their shop that day, Allen stood outside the store. He waited for Michael's usual walk past their shop on the way home for his family's supper time. Allen's voice stopped Michael when in front of him. "Hi. Do you have time for a little talk?"

"Okay Allen. What do you want to talk about?"

"It's about your daughter Nina. She was here today for butter. She's very attractive and very different in many ways from most girls. I ask for your permission to date her."

"She's only fifteen and a half years old. That's too young for her to date anyone."

"Okay, I'll wait until she's old enough to start courting her."

Allen went back into the shop and Michael continued his walk home. While walking, Michael recalled how family of Felix and Allen fit into his wife's [Jean's] family before married. He recalled Linda's grudges against Allen who labelled her daughter Lynn as pampered and spoiled with rejection of her for marriage. He also recalled recent gossip about a growing grudge Felix held against Allen for their business partnership.

Nina waited for her father's return home from his shop. While they sat alone together for the evening meal, Nina told him that Aunt Lucy had her mother send her to the store. She added Tricia's confession to a lie that caused her [Nina] to suffer a beating from their mother.

"Dad, what's going on? Family life for me keeps getting worse."

Michael's first words were an outburst: "Any other form of child labor would be against the law!" He calmed self before he spoke to Nina. "Your sister still doesn't think she'd someday need and want her sister. Nor realize that if she doesn't change, she'll be guilty of more wrongs than any sister could forgive. I've talked to her about this, but it apparently changed nothing. I've done my duty as a father. Only time could tell how things go for your sister bonds."

Aunt Lucy later talked privately with Felix. "Someday I'll help to make Allen suffer

financial loss to even the score for your lost extra income from the business partnership. Let me add that your fixed disability income could continue uninterrupted if you help my work."

"What help do you want from me?"

"For now, you start gossip with your customers that Nina's mother wanted her and Allen to marry each other. And that made your brother ask Nina's father for permission to court her. Later, I'll tell you when to start gossip that Nina flirted with Allen while a customer waiting to be served." [This was before and after Leo was put into family with his brother their chaperone for the two months to Nina's sixteenth birthday.]

Nina and a Personal Diary

Lucy was in her mid-twenties and still never employed. As the last unmarried offspring of her mother, their living expenses were covered by her married brothers, Rocco and Caesar. Lucy had much free time to arrange the lives of family for whatever reason or purpose.

On a Monday morning, Nina was again busy reading a book after younger siblings were in school, Lewis was in his workplace, and their mother left for her waitress work. Aunt Lucy walked around the street block to visit Nina and give her a wrapped package. "This is a gift from me to you."

As Nina unwrapped the package, she asked, "For what occasion? It's not Christmas and not my birthday."

"This is a book without a written story for you to read. It's a book in which *you* write the story. It could be the story about your life but that would be reliving the past and this book should be about onward life. This is called a personal diary. It's what growing girls use to write things that they tell no one, not even a close friend. Writing in this diary is also a way to release thoughts and feelings you're not yet sure about, or that no one wants to hear about. When you begin to write in this diary you must find a place to hide it and tell no one where it's hidden. Not even your family. This way it is always your private, personal property."

"But you'd know I have it, and you are part of my family."

"Only I know because I'm introducing you to a personal diary with a gift of one. And I'm not part of your family that live together in the same place. I must now get back home to finish what was started with grandma. Don't get up; I'll let myself out."

Lucy's maternal uncle Doctor Andrew was her mother's brother. He had a son who was given his name but referred to as Andy instead of junior. Andy also became a physician whose patience called him Doctor Andy. Doctor Andy was a nephew for Lucy's mother [Patricia] and a first cousin for Lucy and her four siblings. Relationship made Doctor Andrew a grand uncle for Nina and her siblings, Doctor Andy a second cousin for Nina and her siblings.

Today, Nina noticed that her mother didn't leave home for her ten o'clock start of waitress work. Nina left home at the usual time for school; on the way she felt a hand on her shoulder and Aunt Lucy's voice: "Your mother doesn't feel well but doesn't show it; she shouldn't be alone today. As the oldest daughter, you should lose today's day in school to be with her now. I'm not able to be any help for your mother today because grandma needs my help with something."

"My mother didn't look or act sick. She didn't leave home for work at the usual time but looked and behaved in her usual ways. I know her workday schedule in the restaurant is sometimes changed."

"Today is not one of those rare times. Your mother doesn't complain with words or actions. She's committed to her duties as wife, mother, and homemaker plus her waitress work to help your family's money needs."

"Why choose me instead of my sister or our older brother? They've had a good and constant relationship with our mother."

"Lewis is a newcomer in his workplace. He'd lose a day's wages and risk the loss of his job if he took a day off work now. It's also not the norm for sons to physically care for their mother. Your sister should never miss a day from school. It's always been hard for her to make average school marks. On the other hand, your school marks are always very high. Tomorrow you could quickly pick up what went on in today's lost day of school."

"I still don't think my mother needs me home with her today."

"Have you ever caught me in a lie? You must learn that nothing and no one comes before a mother. Being with your mother when needed could make her care more about you in return."

Aunt Lucy joined Nina in the walk back home until the corner where Aunt Lucy left Nina and went around the block to her home. When Nina was inside home, she found her mother on the kitchen table with a lot of newspapers below the table and on a nearby chair. Doctor Andy stood by Jean; his Aunt Patricia [Nina's grandma] was near to him with clean towels in her hands. Doctor Andy looked at Nina and faced Jean whom he asked, "What is Nina doing here?"

Jean replied with a surprised voice. "She left for school at the usual time. I don't know why she came back home so soon after she left."

"We'll just have to work with the situation. It has grown more than allowed for this procedure and could not be put off for another time. Nina could help while your mother recovers from the shock of seeing her here."

Nina was still feeling shock at what she witnessed when Doctor Andy told her, "Hand me some of the newspapers on that chair." Nina saw him wrap the fetus in newspaper, announced it was a boy, and went through the back door to put it in the garbage containers. When back in the kitchen, Doctor Andy told Jean. "You say you had a miscarriage. Besides that, remember that this cancels the promise of help for the boy's arm!" He repeated it in Italian for his Aunt Patricia.

Jean replied, "I remember our agreement that this cancels your earlier promise." Jean was off the table and seated on a chair next to her mother. Doctor Andy was packing his medical bag when Nina left the apartment headed for Aunt Lucy. Nina's anger mixed with lingering shock at what she witnessed. Aunt Lucy had just opened the apartment door when Nina's angry voice said, "Why did you lie to me? My mother wasn't sick. Grandma was with my mother instead of here for you to help her with something. You knew my mother was having a procedure that destroyed a life. Why did you make me a witness to it?"

"It was a way to help you know some of the duties for nurses in addition to what you were given in the hospital and its clinic. It was a way to help your decision to someday be a nurse."

"There's nothing more to talked about with you now. I'm going to take a long walk before I go back to where I live." Nina knew today's stress could not make her concentrate in classes for the rest of the school day. When back home, her mother was ready to leave for her waitress work. When Nina was alone, she took the personal diary from her hiding place and sat at the kitchen table with it. She wrote today's experiences and didn't omit a detail, then put it back to her hiding place. Writing about today helped to relieve only some of her mental anguish. She tried to read one of her books to mentally distract her mind from what she witnessed today.

When Nina and her father finished their evening meal together, they left the apartment for another of their walks. This is when Nina told him about today. Michael made no comment about it to her but silently put together what made sense for how the family worked together.

He recalled weeks ago when his brother Lance was in his shop and left a hat to be cleaned. Lance talked about his four-year-old son and two-year-old daughter and how the young children made him feel young --- not too old to be a father. Michael now believed Lucy used Lance to encourage him to have another child as part of the trick to punish Nina for more than one family and more than one reason: Nina's refusal to forget about the convent --- Nina's refusal to replace Lucy as Chester's bride --- and Nina's refusal to be Carlos' bride that caused Lance to lose face and to suffer the anger of his wife and her siblings who counted on it for an end of troubled life from Carlos and his mother. At the same time, Lucy had clean hands punishment for her cousin Doctor Andy with a witness to the illegal abortion that would keep his career work in jeopardy.

The next morning, Nina asked her mother for a note to excuse her absence from school. Jean said "No." as Nina sipped at a cup of coffee and spat what she didn't yet swallow.

Nina asked her mother, "Why does this coffee taste different?"

"I'm trying a different brand of coffee. It's supposed to warm your insides on the way to school."

"It tastes and smells like alcohol!"

"If you think its alcohol, remember that priests drink alcohol from the chalice at the altar when they conduct Mass."

Nina left home for school. She stood at the homeroom teacher's desk to tell her why she didn't have a written excuse for yesterday's absence. Nina barely spoke when the teacher said her breath smelled of alcohol and wanted to know when and where she drank it before coming to class. The teacher refused Nina's words about her mother's use of a different brand of coffee and marked the smell of alcohol on her school record. The teacher added a truancy mark for Nina's absence without a note to excuse it.

The next day, Nina was again alone before her walk to school. She took the diary from its hiding place. She wrote about yesterday's experiences in school and then returned the diary to her hiding place.

On Saturday, Aunt Lucy asked Nina to join her for a long walk. During the walk, Nina heard Aunt Lucy say, "My good-looking educated cousin wouldn't introduce me to eligible, educated bachelors with good looks and a promising good future."

Nina asked, "Why are you telling me this?"

"I'm not telling you anything. As I've said before, I have an uncontrollable habit to think out loud. It's like making the brain work twice, but I'm not telling you anything."

* * * * * * * * * * * *

Michael and his family were in their railroad style apartment less than three months when Doctor Robert was discharged from military service. Doctor Robert was a medical physician in the military and now aimed to start private practice with the start of patients being family, friends and neighbors. Lucy and her mother his patients and insisted that Jean do the same for her family of seven people: "Medically qualified family is too closely bonded to care for and treat members of their own family. Doctor Robert knows much about our personal lives and health issues. It helps him to care for and treat all of us better than other doctors who'd know nothing about us. Becoming patients of Doctor Robert would let him know Nina survived the injuries that he said was not possible."

What Lucy did not remind Jean about now was that Nina's survival would make Doctor Robert remember that she witnessed his medical wrong and could jeopardize his career. As a witness, Nina could also back up her mother if she wanted to make him responsible for her signature on papers that made Nina a medical guinea pig.

Doctor Robert's private practice was open to patients when Nina had another blackout. This time, Jean wanted a medical diagnosis for it and took time off waitress work to take Nina to Doctor Robert. Nina immediately recognized him. She silently recalled him as the man with her mother at the doorway of the hospital room the morning after her accident. Nina remembered that Doctor Robert saw her attempts to show she wasn't in a coma as he told her mother when he asked her to sign the papers. Nina now knew his name and private practice location.

After Doctor Robert's short examination, he told Jean, "I find no medical cause for why Nina blacked out. It could be part of teenage growing years."

After Jean paid his nurse, they walked back home. Nina couldn't remain silent about Doctor Robert: "I don't want Doctor Robert for my medical needs. He didn't keep his oath to *do no harm* years ago when I was in the hospital. He failed his duty to put a patient's comfort and well-being above all else. I heard you tell the hospital nun that you signed the papers and abandoned me there after he made you believe I couldn't survive. That's proof he didn't care about you either. How could you trust him again after then?"

Jean ignored what Nina said. "Your father and I pay the bills! We decide who to make our family doctor and we chose Doctor Robert." When home, Jean was ready for the trip to her waitress work. She made sure Nina had a key to lock their apartment door when she left for school. While alone, Nina took the diary from its hiding place to write today's experiences in it. She added her recollection of Aunt Lucy's words about Doctor Robert not having chosen a bride from his own kind and then returned the diary to the hiding place.

While sleeping that night, Nina woke with the nightmare of her burning dress. Tricia was not in the bed they shared. No family comforted her before she recovered from the nightmare. This seemed to reconfirm the hospital nun's words to Nina that she must always take care of herself and never count on her family to care about her whenever needed.

It was a usual Saturday morning when Nina expected to be home alone for two hours or more. Her mother shopped for groceries in more than one store before back home. Lewis was at his wage paying work for an eight-hour day, and the three younger siblings spent the morning to mid-afternoon with friends in the nearby park.

Nina was with her diary at the kitchen table when she suddenly and unexpectedly heard a key at the apartment front door. She rushed to put the diary back into its hiding place. It was still in her hand when she heard Tricia's voice and then saw her sister enter the kitchen.

"Hi. I came back for what I forgot to take with me to my friend's home. What book is in your hand? Is it something new to read? May I look at it to see what you are now reading?"

"It's not a book that I read. It's a personal diary that Aunt Lucy gave me to write my private feelings, thoughts and experiences into it. Writing in it helps me to feel better as Aunt Lucy said it would."

Tricia interrupted: "Why is the kitchen stove's broiler drawer open? No one in our family has ever used the stove's oven or broiler for anything. Not even our mother."

"That's why it's a perfect hiding place. Clean pots and pans are stored in the oven, but nothing is ever put into the broiler drawer. These stove parts are not like furniture to be dusted, polished or cleaned. It made the broiler drawer a safe hiding place. Now only you know about my diary and where it is hidden. If the diary is ever gone, I could only believe that you took it. If it was stolen, it means that my right to privacy would be lost. This is a different kind of privacy from when you wanted to keep our bedroom as your private room after I was reclaimed from the hospital. My diary and its hiding place are a matter of privacy---my privacy!"

"I was only seven years old when I said those things about our bedroom. I temporarily forgot that sisters should care about and help each other. I'm now fourteen years old and we've been in the same bedroom for years now. Aside from that, why would I or anyone want your personal and private diary? Why would I tell anyone you have a diary or where it is hidden?" Tricia went into the shared bedroom and left the apartment with something in her hand that she didn't let Nina see. After Tricia left, Nina added this experience with her sister to the diary and put it away for the rest of today.

A week after then, Nina was alone and wanted to review what her diary held, but it wasn't in her hiding place. She pulled out the broiler drawer to see if it fell behind or under it but found nothing. She waited for Saturday's family meal. All were seated at the kitchen table when Nina asked, "Has anyone recently used our kitchen stove's oven or broiler?"

Nina looked at everyone's reaction, with the longest look at Tricia who quickly said, "I had nothing to do with your diary not being in stove broiler drawer." Tricia's response now told everyone that she knew about Nina's diary and its hiding place. All other family said they didn't know Nina had a personal diary until now that Tricia mentioned it. Supper time nearly ended when Aunt Lucy arrived and joined the conversation without asking for all that was said beforehand:

"Maybe you made a change in the hiding place, but habit made you look where it used to be. Give yourself time to get over being upset and you might remember your new hiding place. If you go for a walk now it might make you feel relaxed and help you remember."

Nina left from the building front doors. After a long walk alone, she returned home through the kitchen back door. Her gum soled shoes kept her from being heard as she walked through the long alley to the kitchen back door. This six-family structure had a long flight of steps to and from each floor level. Nina was near to the back of the building when she heard the voices of Tricia and Aunt Lucy.

Aunt Lucy's excited voice said, "We've got a goldmine! There's almost nothing we must do without!"

Tricia voice was equally excited. "And life would be kept too busy to remember the past and what's forever gone."

Aunt Lucy said, "Things are right to make the dummy a puppet. All is in our favor!"

Nina followed the sound of their voices to the open space under the building's long stairway to the second floor. Tricia and Aunt Lucy had a temporary look of surprise when Nina asked, "What goldmine are you two talking about? Whose life would be too busy to remember what things? And how does a dummy use a puppet?"

As Nina was approaching them under the stairway, Aunt Lucy put one arm behind her back, and the other arm around Tricia's shoulder and said, "It's something private between us as godmother and godchild that can't be shared with anyone else. Our relationship is as private as the diary is to you. Let your mother see you're back and that we'll also be inside soon."

Aunt Lucy became keeper of Nina's diary to include when and how it would be used. When Nina visited grandma and Aunt Lucy, she would not have the freedom to search their home even if she suspected her diary was with Aunt Lucy

Trapped Nina

A few months before Nina was given the gift of a personal diary, and before it was stolen, her cousin Leslie warned that she "couldn't fight the odds". Leslie told Nina she'd help her with a quick move far from family roots after she gets her education. Family records kept all that Leslie said to Nina, and to all present, before she left rooted family for a different part of the country. Nina had no understanding of what Leslie meant about fighting "the odds"; other family didn't help her to understand it, but she was anxious for when Leslie would help her to also leave family roots.

The Family had arranged Nina to unknowingly be the bride of more than one man --- all who were at an inability to accept another rejection. One who expected her for marriage was for lifelong repeated uses to destroy her religious ways and unblemished life. The Family's mixed work added doctors for Nina's onward troubled life.

In those times, doctors were viewed as if a God. Some doctors were truly concerned about helping patients to regain good health. Some doctors made it an ego trip and social status. Doctors wanted nothing bad on their record and didn't want a damaged reputation for loss of patients. Spouse and family of the doctors were proud to have a doctor among them. Spouse and family shared what shamed the doctor boasted about.

Before Nina's three years out of family life with accident injuries, she was part of family life and nothing about their ways would have shocked her. Since those years away from them caused her to lose memory about family life, she didn't even suspect criminal activity for the family she was forced to return to.

Nina didn't suspect that her stolen diary created opportunities for extortion in addition to jeopardizing the continued career of the two medical doctors.

Nina's handwriting in the diary would be another benefit to the families. It could have been used to practice her handwriting for when forgery would use it however wanted for whatever purpose. Aunt Lucy refused to lend the diary to anyone for any use.

———